CASTONBURY PARK
A Regency Upstairs Downstairs

Survival of the fittest is fine, so long as you're the one on top…but the family that has everything is about to lose it all…

The Montagues have found themselves at the centre of the *ton*'s rumour mill, with lords and ladies alike claiming the family is not what it used to be.

The mysterious death of the heir to the Dukedom, and the arrival of an unknown woman claiming he fathered her son, is only the tip of the iceberg in a family where scandal upstairs *and* downstairs threatens the very foundations of their once powerful and revered dynasty…

D0237979

Montague Family Tree

Hannah Stratton Housekeeper b.1766

Duchess of Rothermere b.1767 d.1800 ⬌ **Duke of Rothermere** b.1758 — **Charles** b.1761 d.1797 ▬ **Claire** b.1787

Adam b.1784

Jamie b.1786

Giles b.1788

Henry (Harry) b.1791

Kate b.1792

Edward b.1796 d.1815

Phaedra b.1796

Ross b.1787

Araminta b.1795

KEY:
⬌ Legal Marriage
— Child
– – Suspected illegitimate child
······ Sibling
▬ Half sibling

Jamie,

*After months of heartache and uncertainty, seeing you
again still leaves a hole in my heart. It's hard for me to
admit, but you're not the son I once knew and, whilst
you bear a physical resemblance to Jamie Montague, I
cannot be certain that you are really him. The pain and
the darkness in your eyes is consuming you. I thought that
learning what had happened would bring this family
closure, but my biggest fear now is that your return to
Castonbury Park will turn a contained scandal into one
that's rapidly getting out of control.*

Father

First published in Great Britain 2012
Mills & Boon, an imprint of Harlequin (UK) Limited,
Eton House, 18-24 Paradise Road, Richmond, Surrey TW9 1SR

ISBN: 978 0 263 90192 4

52-0313

Harlequin (UK) policy is to use papers that are natural, renewable and recyclable products and made from wood grown in sustainable forests. The logging and manufacturing processes conform to the legal environmental regulations of the country of origin.

Printed and bound
by CPI Group (UK) Ltd, Croydon, CR0 4YY

A Stranger at Castonbury

AMANDA MCCABE

MILLS & BOON

Chapter One

Spain, 1814

It was her wedding day. And it was utterly unlike she had ever imagined it.

Catalina Perez Moreno studied her reflection in the small, cracked looking glass as she tried to pin her long, thick dark hair into an elegant twist. The canvas tent was cramped and warm with the dusty evening air outside, filled with a small cot and a trunk, a table littered with nursing supplies. Beyond the dingy white fabric walls she could hear the sounds of a military camp, the shouts and laughter of the men, the rattle of sabres and horses' tack, boots on the hard, dusty earth, the women singing as they cooked supper over the campfires.

No, this was nothing like her first wedding day, when her mother and aunts had dressed her in lace and silk before her father had walked her down the aisle of the grand cathedral in Seville to meet her bridegroom. A groom twenty years older than herself who she had met only twice before that day. *That* wedding day had been grand, momentous—and terrifying, disappointing.

This day was different in every way. Her first husband was dead now, as were her parents and brother, and the home she had once known in Seville was long gone thanks to the French invasion of her homeland. She had been alone for many months, using her nursing skills to help the armies trying to drive out those hated French. Alone—until she had looked across the camp one day and seen James Montague, Lord Hatherton.

'Jamie,' Catalina whispered, and then laughed at herself for the warm glow just saying his name created. She had met so many men in her work, moving from camp to camp, hospital to hospital. Men who were handsome and flirtatious, who made her smile, who danced with her, who told her tales of faraway England. But no one had ever made her feel like Jamie did, from that first moment.

He was tall and lean and so very handsome, like a knight from some medieval poem who fought dragons and won the fair hands of beautiful *infantas*. He had seemed not quite real. His dark, glossy hair, carelessly brushed back from his face, had gleamed in the bright sunlight, and beneath the light growth of beard on his jaw he had a chiselled, aristocratically elegant face. His uniform tunic had been unfastened to reveal the thin linen of his shirt, clinging to his muscled chest. He had been so beautiful.

But more than that, he had seemed so full of a burning, vibrant *life*. He'd thrown back his head to laugh at something another man had said to him, and his whole face had seemed lit from within by some vital, sun-bright force. Catalina had been mesmerised, the pile of laundry she'd been carrying falling to the dust. The whole crowded camp had seemed to vanish in that moment, and all she'd been able to see was him. All she'd wanted to do was fall into his laughter, his life.

Then suddenly he had looked right at her, his piercing, pale grey eyes so vivid. His laughter had faded, and she'd felt like such a fool to be caught staring like that. She was a widow, a nurse who had seen so much of the ugly side of life, not a virginal schoolgirl to gape and blush at a handsome man. She had grabbed up the laundry and spun around to run away.

She hadn't got far when she'd felt a hand on her arm, warm and hard through her thin sleeve, and even without turning around she had known it was him. And when he had spoken to her in Spanish, smiled at her, she had been utterly lost.

That was a month ago now. And tonight she would marry him.

Catalina pushed another pin into the heavy strands of her hair, as if that could drive away the imagined sound of her mother's disapproving voice. *Catalina Maria Isabella, what are you thinking to marry a man you know so little of! An Englishman too. It is a disgrace. His family will never accept you, just as we could never accept him. ...*

And Catalina knew all too well how right her mother would be. Jamie was the Marquis of Hatherton, heir to the Duke of Rothermere, and she was a Spanish lady of an old family name but no money since the arrival of the French. No home at all either, since her brother had died defending his liberal politics against the king. They were marrying in secret now so he would be able to prepare his family properly once they returned to England after the war. She knew little of Jamie beyond stolen kisses on walks along the river, whispered conversations beside campfires in the darkness.

But she knew things now her mother had never had to face. She had seen blood and death and destruction. She knew how quickly life, precious time, could flee. And she knew how Jamie made her feel. As if he had every beautiful thing of life in his strong hands. And that was why she had so eagerly said yes when he'd asked her to marry him on one of those sun-dappled walks. Because to her, Jamie Montague *was* life. He was…everything.

'You are doing the right thing,' she told herself. Her reflection stared back at her, her wide, uncertain brown eyes, the sun freckles splashed over her nose. As she pushed in the last pin, the sapphire ring on her finger caught the dying sunlight. Jamie's mother's ring, which he had slid onto her finger when he had asked her to marry him, sparkled. It was an oval sapphire, inscribed inside the gold band with the motto of the Montagues—*Validus Superstes*.

This *was* the right thing. She was seizing her happiness while she could.

Catalina stepped back and smoothed the skirt of her simple white muslin gown. She picked up the white lace mantilla from her trunk and swept it over her hair. She was marrying far from home, with none of her family, but she would go to Jamie looking as much like a proper Spanish bride as she could.

This was their time, and she would seize it with both hands. She would hold on to it for as long as she could.

She heard the sound of booted footsteps on the hard-packed dirt outside. 'Catalina,' Jamie called quietly. 'Are you ready?'

Catalina's heart leapt, and she felt that warm rush of excitement through her that always came when he was near. She caught up her prayer book and answered, '*Sí, mi amor*—I am ready.'

Jamie pushed back the flap of the tent and stepped inside. The sunset outside limned him in a fiery red-orange glow. For an instant, Catalina's eyes were dazzled and she could barely see him. He seemed very far away, as if he stood poised on the edge of another world, one where she could not follow. As if he would fall back into some dark chasm and be lost to her even as she desperately reached out for him.

Don't be so dramatic, she told herself sternly. She had once had a nursemaid who was full of old superstitions and would warn Catalina of all the things that could bring bad fortune at weddings— not crying before the nuptial kiss, forgetting to wear a lump of sugar in the bridal glove, all of which would cause a lifetime of misery. She had terrified Catalina so much that she had feared to make any move at all, until her mother had dismissed the nurse and scoffed at such warnings.

Catalina hadn't thought of such things in years, but today felt so very strange with that blood-red sunset and her heart about to burst. She couldn't help but fear that her feelings for Jamie were too much.

Jamie let the tent flap drop behind him. Without that fiery light surrounding him, Catalina saw that he was only a man, of real flesh and blood.

Not a god or a spirit who would vanish when she touched him. But still she couldn't quite breathe when she looked at him. She couldn't even move. She could only gaze at him and marvel that he was here with her.

He wore his dress uniform, the buttons bright and shimmering against the fine red cloth, his boots polished to a high gloss. His hair, still damp from a washing, waved back from his face, revealing the sculpted angles of his features. She had seldom seen him looking so grand, not amid the rough and tumble of a camp constantly on the move. He looked every inch the fine English nobleman.

Except for his eyes. They were such a light, piercing blue-grey in the shadows and seemed to devour her as he looked at her.

'Catalina,' he said, and his usually velvet-smooth, deep voice was rough. 'How beautiful you are.'

Catalina made herself laugh, even as those simple words made her want to cry. She knew she was *not* beautiful. She was tall and thin, her skin tanned by the sun, her hands roughened by her nursing work. But when Jamie said it, when he looked at her that way—she could almost believe it. She could almost believe she was worthy of him. Just for tonight.

'No, Catalina,' Jamie said. Suddenly he was beside her, taking her hands in his. His touch was warm and strong on her, turning her to face him. 'I can see what you're thinking. You *are* beautiful. The most beautiful woman I've ever seen. I knew that from the first moment I saw you.'

'Oh, Jamie.' Catalina raised their joined hands and pressed a soft kiss to the back of his sunbrowned fingers. Like hers, his hands were scraped and scarred from their lives in camp. There was a thin line of white encircling his smallest finger, the mark of his family's gold signet ring, which he had lost. But his hands were long and elegant, as aristocratic as the rest of him.

'I felt I knew you from that first moment as well,' she said. 'As if I had always known you. How can that be?'

'Because we were meant to find each other,' he answered. He twined his fingers with hers and held her hands against his chest. Beneath the fine red wool, she could feel the rhythm of his heart, steady and reassuring. Precious.

'My family didn't want me to come here,' he said. 'And they were quite right to say I have duties at home, that I shouldn't go off searching for adventure. But something told me I *had* to go, that I couldn't stay still. Not yet.'

Catalina laughed, for it was that very spirit, that energy and life, that drew her to him. 'It is true, Jamie. You are a restless spirit. I never see you still for a moment.'

'Only when I'm with you,' he said. Catalina looked up into his eyes and saw how very serious he was in that instant. 'When I'm with you, I feel peace like I've never known before. This is a terrible place we're in, Catalina, full of death and treachery. But with you…I see none of it any more. I only see your goodness. I don't want to wander or seek when I'm with you. I wish…' His voice broke off and he shook his head, as if words vanished.

'I know,' Catalina said. Her throat ached as if she would cry, sob with all the happiness and fear that was trapped inside of her. 'Oh, Jamie, I know. If we could only stay like this, have it always be like this moment…'

Jamie pressed a soft kiss to her wrist, just where her pulse beat. 'But the chaplain waits for us.'

'We don't have to go, you know,' Catalina said as she thought of his words about his family—they had not wanted him to come here, and quite rightly so. What would they say if he returned to them with her? 'We don't have to marry to be together as we are now.'

'Don't have to marry?' Jamie's eyes narrowed and his hands tightened on hers, as if he thought she might fly away from him. 'Catalina, don't you see? I've finally found you. I don't want you just for a day or an hour. I want you always. I can't let you go.'

'Oh, Jamie.' She felt the hot tears well up in her eyes and she couldn't hold them back any longer. They fell onto her cheeks and she shook her head. 'I want you for always too. I never thought such a thing was possible. But it…frightens me.'

His hands held her even closer. 'I frighten you?'

'No, never you. But the way I feel, it will surely explode inside me. I feel like I'll burst with it when I look at you. Such things can't last.'

'Then we need to hold on to it when we find it.' Jamie's arms came around her and he pulled her against him. 'This is life, Catalina, and it's ours right now. Please don't send me away. Please be my wife. Once this war is over and we can return to England, I vow I will spend the rest of my life making you happy.'

To be his wife—it was all she could want. But still she wanted to cry and she didn't even know why. She wrapped her arms around his neck and held on tightly. She breathed deeply of his citrus-sharp cologne, of that smell that was only Jamie, and she knew she would always remember it. That it would always remind her of this one night when he was hers.

'If you are sure,' she whispered, 'then I will marry you.'

He pressed a kiss to her brow, and she felt the curve of his lips against her as he smiled. 'Then let's go to the church.'

Catalina nodded, and Jamie took her hand to lead her from the tent. The sun had sunk low to the horizon and was just a thin line of glowing red-orange along the edge of the dusky purple sky. The camp was settling down for the night. Only a few people still moved about between the rows of tents, women stirring pots over the fires, men cleaning their weapons and talking together quietly.

Later, when the ale and wine had been flowing, more people would come out to laugh and play music, dance, tell ribald jokes or grow melancholy about faraway homes. But for now everything was calm, and there was no one to pay attention to Catalina and Jamie as they made their way along the roadway.

Catalina caught a glimpse of two people walking in the opposite direction, laughing and chattering. She recognised Mrs Chambers, wife of Colonel Chambers. As usual the lady was rather elaborately dressed for camp life, in a blue silk gown trimmed with blond lace and silk roses, her hair piled in curls atop her head. She was laughing with the red-haired man who walked beside her, Hugh Webster, a man Catalina did not much care for. His eyes were always too cold, too speculative, when he looked at her, and she avoided him whenever she could.

Behind them scurried Mrs Chambers's companion, Alicia Walters. Unlike her employer, Alicia was simply dressed, her pale golden hair pinned up in a tight knot. She always seemed so quiet, so intent on fading into the shadows, but Catalina rather liked her on the rare occasions they'd met. Alicia was polite and refined, kind.

Alicia glanced at Catalina now and gave a quick nod before she looked away. Catalina noticed that Alicia's gaze slid over Jamie and she blushed.

But Catalina had no time to think about anyone else. Jamie's hand closed tight on hers and he led her beyond the edge of the camp, where the horses and carts were kept for the night. The dying sunlight and the flicker of the torches from the middle of camp lit their way along the narrow, rutted path that led to a small, half-abandoned village.

The biggest structure in the darkened town was the chapel, set apart by itself at the end of the lane. Its white stone walls glowed in the shadows like a welcoming beacon, and tonight candlelight shone through the narrow stained-glass windows. Shards of bright red, yellow, green and the vivid blue of the Virgin's robes were cast down onto the ground. The doors stood open as if in welcome for this strange wedding.

Catalina suddenly hesitated. Part of her longed to run forward into that church and throw herself into the future, whatever it held. But there was a part of her, buried deep down inside, that whispered to her to turn back. That warned her.

Jamie's hand on hers, so warm and strong, held her where she was. No matter what waited beyond that threshold, she was no longer alone. She had someone beside her who was willing to leap forward into the chasm with her.

Hand in hand, they climbed the stone steps and made their way into the church. Catalina sometimes went there at quiet moments, to pray for the souls of her family or just to think, away from the crowds and constant clamour of camp. Tonight it looked like a completely different place. Dozens of candles were lit along the carved white altar and beneath the windows, making the small space into a glowing, mysterious fairyland. Bunches of wildflowers splashed their colours into the dusty gloom. Before the altar waited the regiment's chaplain and two of Jamie's fellow officers as well as a Spanish laundress to be witnesses.

Catalina feared she might start to cry yet again. She had gone for so many months being strong, living with what fate had dealt her, stepping carefully from one day to the next. And now she had cried so many times in one day! Her wedding day—the day that should have no tears at all.

She turned to Jamie, and found him smiling down at her. 'You did this?' she whispered.

His smile widened. 'I did. I gathered every candle and every flower I could find. I scoured the countryside for them. Do you like it?'

'Of course I like it! But…why? When did you have time?'

'Because I can't give you what you truly deserve, Catalina,' he answered. 'A fine wedding at the Castonbury church with all my family to see. A satin gown, a cake, a carriage covered with flowers. But I wanted to make this place beautiful for you. A place we can always remember.'

Holding on to his hand, Catalina glanced around the transformed church again. She knew she would never, ever forget the way it looked, in this one still, perfect moment. She would never forget the man beside her and how he felt holding her hand.

'I can't imagine any place more beautiful,' she said softly.

'Then shall we get married?' Jamie said with a

teasing lilt to his voice. Catalina was glad to hear it—he was so very serious too often.

She smiled up at him and nodded. 'Oh, yes. Let's do that. We can't let this beautiful church go to waste.'

And they walked together to the altar and held hands as they said the vows that would bind them together for ever. Or for as long as they lived in such dangerous days.

Chapter Two

Catalina felt it before she saw it, the slight tremble of the earth under their feet as they walked back from the church. Then a fork of sizzling, blue-white lightning split the dark sky above their heads. A rolling rumble of thunder followed, ending in a deafening drumbeat.

'I think the days of drought might be over,' she said. She tipped her head back to peer up at the sky from beneath the lace pattern of her mantilla. The stars and moon that had just begun to peek out as they walked to the church were now hidden beneath drifts of charcoal-grey clouds.

'Just in time for us to move out,' Jamie's friend said wryly. 'Nothing like moving camp in the middle of a rainstorm.'

'Moving camp?' Catalina glanced over at

Jamie. She had heard nothing of any plans to move out. Where were they going now? Could she even follow him there, her new husband, or were they to be parted already?

Jamie gave her a reassuring smile and squeezed her hand. 'We have no orders yet. We have to make the push to Toulouse soon, but there is nothing definite.'

Catalina nodded, but inside she felt that cold touch of disquiet. Her life in the past few months had been nothing but moving, going wherever her nursing skills were needed, wherever she had to be in this strange new life. But she didn't want to be away from Jamie yet.

Not yet.

When they made their way into camp amid the rumble of thunder, it looked to be the usual sort of evening. Men sitting around the fires and outside their tents, talking, laughing, playing cards, passing the long hours. Sometimes Colonel Chambers would host a dinner party or there would be dancing, but tonight everyone seemed to be in a quieter mood. Catalina could hear the strains of some sad ballad in the distance, and it added to the melancholy mood of the approaching storm.

As they passed by the largest tent, the one used for dining and officers' meetings, Chambers stepped outside and called to Jamie.

'Hatherton,' he said. 'May I speak with you for a moment?'

The man was usually all blustery good humour, not as vivacious as his wife but friendly and cheerful, handsome in his pale English way. But tonight he seemed unusually sombre, and that touch of disquiet inside Catalina grew like an icicle, freezing her heart.

'Certainly, Colonel Chambers,' Jamie answered. He kissed Catalina's hand and said quietly, 'I will meet you at my tent as soon as I can—Lady Hatherton.'

Lady Hatherton—how strange it sounded. How foreign. Could it ever truly belong to her? Would it ever feel like it was hers? Yet Jamie's grey eyes warmed her, reassured her, and she smiled at him. No matter how strange his English title sounded, he was just Jamie, and that was the important thing. The only thing.

'Of course,' she said. 'You must attend to your business. I will wait for you there.'

As Catalina left Jamie, she caught a glimpse of

a flutter of pale fabric beside the tent. She looked up and saw that it was Alicia Walters. The woman hovered beside the canvas wall, and Catalina was shocked to see the streak of tears on her cheeks before she spun around and hurried away.

Catalina glanced back at the closed flap of the tent. It opened a crack, just enough for her to see most of the regiment's officers gathered around a table scattered with maps. For an instant she considered running after Alicia and making the woman tell what she knew, but Alicia had vanished into the night.

Catalina quickly made her way to Jamie's tent, which was set almost to the edge of the camp. It was quiet there, darker, almost as if they had a space all to themselves. It was also larger than hers, she saw as she stepped inside. The bed was more spacious, and there was a table piled with locked document cases and ringed with folding camp stools. He had decorated it much like the church, with candles and bouquets of flowers that made the dusty, warm air smell sweet and disguised the harsh, masculine military lines of the room.

The sheets on the bed were crisp and clean,

turned back to reveal flower petals scattered across it in a bright pattern. It made Catalina smile and shiver at the same time to see it, to imagine lying with Jamie there as the flowers clung to their bare skin.

She turned away from the bed and went to the shaving stand. Jamie's combs and brushes were neatly arrayed there, along with a small pastel portrait of two girls she knew were his sisters, Kate and Phaedra. Their blue-grey eyes, so like Jamie's, gleamed with laughter and mischief as they looked out from the frame. She knew Jamie had other siblings and a father, the duke, still living in England, but this was the only personal memento in the tent.

Catalina unpinned her mantilla and carefully folded it before she pulled the combs from her hair and let the heavy, dark mass fall over her shoulders. The thunder was louder now, a steady roar too much like cannon fire, and she could hear the first beats of raindrops against the canvas.

She folded back the flap and peered out into the night. In the distance she could see the lights from the large tent where Jamie was, but then a flash of sparkling lightning split the darkness and for a second she was blinded. She closed her eyes against the light and shivered.

It was a strange night, almost unreal. She could scarcely believe what she had just done. She had married Jamie, and now she was waiting for him, her husband. The darkness, the storm, the shivering anticipation of what was coming, seemed to enclose her in a dream. The whole world had gone mad around her—why should she not be mad too?

Catalina let her head fall back as she listened to the rain batter against the tent and the earth outside, as she inhaled the sweet musky scent of the storm. The rain fell in earnest now, a true storm, and inside her chest her heart seemed to pound louder than the thunder. She turned away from the rain and let the flap fall closed. The sound was muffled now, and she felt almost as if she was enclosed in a cave alone, away from the real world. She sat down on the edge of the bed, and the scent of clean, sun-warmed sheets and flowers rose around her.

She smiled, and then laughed aloud. *Mad indeed.* She fell back into the soft pillows and let the rain and the night surround her. She had a flashing memory of her first wedding night, which had been in a grand, carved bed hung with velvet curtains and spread with silk sheets. A bed that had been in her husband's family since the 1500s, laden with tradition and expectations.

She had been a scared girl then, shy and obedient, and her husband had done nothing to soothe her fears. When he died, she had thought she would never marry again, never be bound to someone like that. And when her brother died, she ran away from Seville to be a nurse, and the feeling of freedom was wondrous despite the dangers. She had never wanted to give that up.

Until Jamie. He had changed everything.

Catalina rolled onto her side and hugged Jamie's pillow to her. She had never met anyone like him before, so intriguing, so full of life. He made her behave in ways she could never have imagined, ways that were wild and impulsive. He made her feel *alive*, and she would revel in that for every moment she could.

She held on to the pillow and fancied its linen folds still smelled of Jamie. The patter of the rain lulled her into a half waking, half asleep dream state.

Suddenly she heard a soft rustling sound, as if a cloth was being shifted. The bed moved as someone sat down beside her and a hand gently touched her hip through the thin linen of her chemise.

She started to turn over, but Jamie whispered, 'Shh. I didn't mean to wake you.'

'I was waiting for you,' she said.

He eased her hair away from the side of her neck and she felt his kiss on the soft skin just below her ear. She shivered at the delicious sensation of it, and his lips slid down her neck to caress her shoulder. His hand moved along her body, and she could feel the hunger in his touch. A hunger that echoed her own.

She rolled over to wrap her arms around him and pull him up against her. Their mouths met in a kiss full of desperate desire. She needed him so much, and she wanted him to need her too. Wanted only the two of them in their own small world for just a little while longer.

She felt his hands close hard around her waist and he turned in one quick movement so that she lay on top of him. His tongue traced the curve of her lower lip, lightly, teasingly, before he slid deep inside.

Desire gathered around her like a blurry, heated cloud, and she felt his hand on her backside, dragging her tight against him. She arched her hips into his hard erection and spread her legs wider over him.

He groaned hoarsely, and their kiss slid into wild, frantic need. He had already removed his coat, and she tore at the lacings of his shirt until she could touch his bare skin. She pressed her palms to his chest, revelling in the hot, smooth feeling of his skin over those lean muscles. His breath, his heartbeat, his strength—how she loved all of it.

'Catalina,' he whispered. 'Please, I need you. I need to see you.'

Catalina sat up, her knees braced to either side of his hips. He watched her with burning bright grey eyes as she untied the ribbon at the neck of her chemise. She drew it up over her head and let it fall away.

'I've never seen anything as beautiful as you,' he said.

'No,' she argued. 'Nothing is as beautiful as

you.' She traced her fingertips over the bare skin of his chest. Lightly, she touched the sharp curve of his hip, the line of his lean thigh—the hard heat of his manhood through his breeches.

'Catalina,' he growled. In one swift movement, he knelt before her. His hands at her waist dragged her tight against him until not a single breath could come between them.

He kissed her fiercely, and she felt his touch on her naked breast. His roughened palm slid beneath it to cradle its weight, and his long fingers teased at her hardened nipple, a soft, fleeting caress. He teased her until she moaned and arched her back to press herself against him. He finally gave her what she longed for, rolling the sensitive nipple hard between his fingers.

Her desire burned even higher at his touch. She held tightly to his shoulders, digging her fingers deep into his skin to hold him with her. He slid down her body until his mouth closed over her nipple, sucking deeply.

Catalina's head fell back weakly as she cried out incoherent Spanish words, begging for yet more of him. He seemed hungry for her too. His open mouth trailed along her skin to her stomach, his tongue circling her navel as his hand curled hard around the back of her thigh and tugged her closer to him. He pressed a kiss softly to the inside of her leg and one finger eased along the seam of her womanhood and slid inside of her.

'Jamie,' she panted. Her eyes closed tightly as she concentrated on every touch. Suddenly she felt his tongue touch her *there.* 'Jamie, no!'

'Shh, let me,' he whispered, and she gave herself over to what he did to her, what he made her feel. He tasted her so deeply she could have no secrets from him. Waves of burning pleasure washed over her and she fell down into them. She drove her fingers into his hair and held him to her—she wanted more and more, she wanted all of him.

Her climax took hold of her, low at her very core, a building, burning pressure. She let it expand over her whole body until every coherent thought vanished and there was only feeling. Only him. As he thrust his tongue deep within her one more time she exploded.

'Jamie,' she breathed as she sank down to the bed, her legs spread as he knelt between them. He stared down at her, his grey eyes so dark they seemed almost black, his chest heaving with the force of his breath.

Catalina reached out to unfasten his breeches and push them away from his hips. He was hard with his own unfulfilled desire, velvet over hot iron, beckoning for her touch and she gave in to the temptation. She ran her hand slowly up his length and down again and he trembled at her caress. His erection strained against her hand, yet he held very, very still.

'Catalina,' he whispered harshly.

She sat up and pushed him down in her place so she could strip away his breeches and see the beauty of his naked body at last. The light from the fires through the canvas walls of the tent turned his skin to gold, and she touched every inch of him, wondering that he could be her husband.

'Catalina, I can't bear this much longer,' he said as he reached up to caress her hair. She bent her head to kiss his shoulder, to bite lightly at his flat brown nipple. Suddenly he seized her by the hips and rolled her down to the bed as he rose up above her. He buried his face in the curve of her neck and shoulder, kissing her skin as she wrapped her arms around him and laughed out of sheer happiness.

'Do you want me, Catalina?' he whispered. 'Do you want me inside you?'

'Yes,' she cried. She opened herself to him and he slid deeply into her, home at last. She wrapped her legs around him and closed her eyes as she felt him with her.

He drew back only to drive forward again and again, a delicious friction rough and hot inside of her. She listened to the harsh, uneven rhythm of his breath as they moved together, seeking their pleasure. He was part of her now, but she wanted everything he could give—and she wanted to give him everything in return.

Faster and faster they moved, their cries mingling. She rose up and caught his lips with hers as she felt her climax build again. She cried out at the sudden release, a shower of white and glowing blue sparks that seemed to fall over her. His back tightened under her touch, and he arched back as he shouted out her name.

He fell heavily to the bed beside her, facedown as he trembled. Catalina was shaking too, exhausted and exalted by the pleasure of their lovemaking. By the sheer joy of being with Jamie. She opened her eyes to stare up at the canvas ceiling above them, breathing slowly and deeply until she could float back down to earth again. She smiled, feeling so wonderfully free. So perfectly where she should be.

Jamie wrapped his arm around her waist and hugged her close as she turned on her side with her back pressed to his chest. She ran her fingertips over his arm as she listened to the sound of his breath mingle with the night breeze outside.

'Tell me a tale,' she said softly.

Jamie chuckled sleepily. 'What sort of tale?'

'One of your home.'

'I have told you about Castonbury already!'

Catalina laughed. 'I want to hear it again. I want to know everything about you.' Just as he knew her stories of her own life—her parents and their cold, correct home; her brother, lost fighting against a tyrannical king; her first marriage, so brief and so disappointing. She much preferred to hear about England and his family there.

Jamie laughed. 'I don't think you would want to know everything. You might not like me so much then.'

'Never!' Catalina protested. 'Your home cannot be so awful. From what you have told me it sounds beautiful.'

'Castonbury *is* beautiful, in its own terrible way.' Jamie kissed her hair, but she could hear from the faraway note in his voice that he was somewhere else in his mind for the moment. 'When I was a child I thought it was its own world, a playground for me and my siblings. We ran over the fields, fished and rowed on the lakes, played hide-and-seek behind the marble columns. Chased one another in front of gilded mirrors and under Waterford glass chandeliers and frescoed rotundas. We never realised how grand it all was.'

'It sounds like a palace,' Catalina murmured, trying to picture it all in her mind. Her own family's home in Seville was ancient and filled with heirlooms from her relatives, but it was all crumbling and faded, past its grand days.

'It was built to make everyone think that, to awe every visitor with how spectacular the Montague family has been. To make them think they have been transported to the villa of a Roman emperor.' Jamie pressed a soft kiss to her bare shoulder. 'It's beautiful, but it is also deeply lonely.'

'Is that why you left it? Why you came here?'

'A person can so easily get lost at Castonbury and never find themselves at all. Perhaps that is why I came to Spain.'

'To find yourself?'

'To find you.' Jamie turned her in his arms until she lay on her back, gazing up at him in the shadows. 'Did *you* come here to find yourself?'

Catalina laughed. 'I think I came here to escape. Bandaging wounds seemed much preferable to living as a proper Spanish widow, all swathed in black. My house never felt like a home either, not after my brother died.'

Her brother—he had been a brave man, willing to risk all for his belief in a constitution for Spain, a country free of tyranny and a better version of itself. Until he'd fallen foul of a king who wanted the exact opposite, and was willing to deal with the French to gain his ends. No, Seville had never been a home once he was gone.

'So we have found a home in each other,' Jamie said.

'Yes,' Catalina said, even as she shivered with

a sudden jolt of fear. For however long this happiness lasted, it was perfect.

And then he kissed her, and everything else disappeared.

Jamie gently smoothed a lock of Catalina's dark hair back from her face and watched her as she slept. A small smile curved her lips, as if she was in a good dream, and her cheeks were flushed a pretty pale pink.

She was so beautiful. A gift he had never looked for when he came to Spain. A gift he had never expected in his life. He feared to hold it too tightly, as if it would shatter like a fine-spun glass ornament, but he never wanted to lose it. All his life he had felt alone, even in the midst of a house crowded with family and servants. But now, as he held Catalina, that feeling vanished. He had spoken the truth to her—in moments like this he had an inkling of what home could mean.

So how could he tell her what he had been asked to do for the English government? How they had assigned him to help bring the Spanish king back to his throne. How could he tell her this after what had happened to her brother, and given what she herself believed?

Catalina murmured in her sleep, and Jamie held her close until she grew quiet again. He wished he could just hold her like this until every ugly thing vanished for her, until he could make her life perfect. But he knew he could not.

He would have to keep her safe the only way he knew how. Through his work.

Smoke billowed around her, acrid and choking, so thick she could see nothing. She could hear the crackle of flames, the crash of burning wood around her, but she was lost in that terrible cloud.

And she was alone. Catalina held out her hands, grasping for something, anything. 'Jamie!' she cried out. There was no answer, and as she stumbled forward she suddenly fell into a bottomless, endlessly dark pit. She was falling and falling. ...

Catalina sat straight up, her heart pounding. For an instant she wasn't sure what was real and what she had dreamed, if those hazy, half-seen terrors were real. She drew in a deep breath of air scented with rain and Jamie's cologne and then she remembered the wedding, the storm. Being held safe in Jamie's arms.

She glanced to the other side of the bed. It was empty, but the sheets were still rumpled. As she ran her fingertips over the cool softness of the linen, she heard a soft rustle from across the tent. She looked over her shoulder to see Jamie sitting at the table with papers scattered in front of him, his back to her. His dark head was bent over the documents, and he wore his breeches but no shirt. The candlelight flickered and glowed over his smooth skin, carving the lean, muscled lines into hard marble.

For a moment Catalina just looked at him, drinking in every part of him as she remembered how his hands felt on her, how his body felt as it moved over hers. She suddenly had the terrible feeling that she wanted to seize on to this moment and never let it go, that she had to remember it always.

Suddenly Jamie seemed to sense that she watched him. His shoulders grew tense, and he turned to look at her. His pale grey eyes, those eyes that seemed to see everything, pierced into hers and she shivered at the intensity she saw in their depths.

But then he smiled, and it was almost as if a new light broke through the storm. 'You should sleep a little longer,' he said. 'It's a few hours yet until dawn.'

'You should sleep too,' Catalina said. 'You have been working too hard lately, planning this push to Toulouse.'

Jamie shook his head and a lock of dark hair fell over his brow. He shook it back impatiently and looked back down at the papers before him. 'The planning may be done now,' he muttered.

A tiny sliver of ice seemed to touch Catalina's heart at those quiet words. She reached for his discarded shirt at the foot of the bed and pulled it over her head. 'What do you mean? Are we really moving out soon?'

'Very soon,' he said. He rubbed his hand over his jaw. 'Within the next couple of days.'

'But…the rain,' Catalina said softly. She could still hear the storm outside, the water that flowed over the canvas of the tent. She knew what such sudden storms were like when they came to break the dry weather, how violent and swift they were. 'We'll have to cross the Bidasoa.'

'I may not be with you by then,' Jamie said, and his voice was so distant, so eerily, coolly calm. He hardly seemed like the passionate, maddened lover who had rolled with her across this very bed only an hour ago.

Still feeling cold, Catalina pushed back the sheets and slid out of bed. The faded old carpet felt prickly under her bare feet and the air was cold and clammy from the rain, but she hardly noticed as she slowly walked across the tent. All she could see was Jamie.

He pushed the papers he was looking at back into their case as she stopped beside the table.

'Where are you going?' she asked. 'Somewhere dangerous?' She felt foolish even as she said the words. *Of course* he was going someplace dangerous—that was their lives in Spain now, and a man like Jamie, an English officer, was always at the very heart of it.

Yet she had a strange feeling there was more to this than the usual marching and shooting, more than the danger they faced every day. Her glance flickered to the hidden papers. 'You are leaving the regiment?'

'For a time.' Jamie ran his hands over his face again, and Catalina had the sense that he wrestled with something deep inside, something he couldn't or wouldn't share with her. Somewhere she couldn't yet follow.

She knelt beside him and took his hands tightly in hers. She could feel the scrapes and calluses of his hands, the warmth of his skin against hers. 'I am your wife now,' she said quietly. 'You can share anything with me, Jamie, and it will be safe. I will follow you anywhere.'

'Oh, Catalina.' He smiled down at her, but she could still see that shadow in his eyes. He turned his hand in hers and raised her fingers to his lips for a lingering, tender kiss. 'There are places where I would never let you follow me.'

Catalina curled her fingertips lightly around his cheek. His evening growth of dark beard tickled her palm and she smiled. 'How would you stop me?'

Jamie smiled wryly against her hand. 'I couldn't, of course. No one is braver or more stubborn than you.'

'Except for you?'

'I can be stubborn indeed when it comes to keeping you safe.' He held out her hand balanced on his and studied the way her fingers twined with his. 'Would you not consider going to my family in England?'

Catalina fell back on her heels, so surprised by his words that she didn't know what to say. 'England? But…I have never been there. Your family wouldn't know me.' She would be a foreigner in an English home centuries old. Yes, she had found it within herself to leave her home and come here to be a nurse—but at least she knew Spain, knew the people. In England would she not be alone?

'They would come to know you—and you would be safe there until I could join you.'

If he could join her there. The unspoken words hung heavy between them, and Catalina felt a bolt of pure fear. She had known Jamie would have to go at some time, that everything that was happening around them would part them. But not yet. *Please God, not yet.*

She pulled herself to her feet and sat down heavily on the other stool. Her hands fell from

Jamie's, and he leaned closer to her, his forearms braced on his knees. 'What is happening, Jamie?' she said. 'What is in those papers?'

'I've been requested to take on a secret assignment,' Jamie said quietly.

'Secret?' Catalina said, confused. 'What does that mean?'

'I have done such tasks before, when a certain degree of...discretion is required. It turns out I am unfortunately rather good at subterfuge.'

'What have they asked you to do this time?'

Jamie silently reached for the papers. 'You must understand, I have told no one else about this. Utter secrecy is necessary. But you should know.'

Catalina nodded. He handed her the documents and she quickly scanned them. As she read, a growing sense of disbelief and dismay crept over her. 'It—it looks as if you are to work for King Ferdinand.'

'Not for him. For the English forces who see it as being in their best interests for him to return to the throne.'

'And you are merely their pawn? You, a marquis?'

'It is not quite like that.' He took the papers

gently from her numb hands and locked them back in the box. 'I have done such things before when the need arose. But it is different now.'

'Different how?' Catalina demanded, still so confused and angry. Jamie was her husband now, but did she really know him so little? Was her husband only a figure of her imagining, and was a cold English nobleman the truth?

No—she could not believe that of Jamie. Never. But why would he undertake such a task?

'Different because of you. Because of all you have told me, about your family and your brother.' He reached for her hand and she let him take it. 'Because I know I must be more careful now.'

Catalina shook her head, biting back a sob. 'Yes, you do have to be more careful, for so many reasons. I know how terrible war is, how so much can change so quickly—but I do not want to lose you.' Not now, when she felt as if she was first coming to know him. Not now, when she had to make him see things from her point of view.

But how would they make it all work after the war was over, and they had to find a normal way of life together?

'I never want to lose you either.' He raised her

hand to his lips and kissed her fingers. 'I couldn't bear it, not now that I have just found you.'

'So you will not take this task?'

He didn't answer. Instead he stood and drew her up into his arms. He pulled her closer and his lips came down on hers in a hungry, hot kiss. A kiss that said he would never let her go, and Catalina wanted to believe it. She never wanted to let him go either. Despite everything that seemed to stand between them now, she had never felt for anyone what she did for Jamie. Surely she never could again.

They fell together to the rumpled blankets of the bed, their bodies entwined. And for that moment it was all that mattered—even as she knew one moment could not last for ever.

When Catalina woke again, the rain was gone and watery sunlight pierced through the canvas walls of the tent. The air was growing warm, and she could hear the tumult of shouts and running footsteps from outside. It was day, and something was happening out there.

And Jamie was not with her. She was alone in the tent.

Catalina quickly pushed herself out of bed and grabbed her work clothes out of her trunk. The lace mantilla fluttered from the edge of the table like a ghost, a memory that seemed far away even though she had worn it only last night. She tucked it carefully into the depths of the trunk and hastily twisted her hair up into a tight knot.

As she dressed, she remembered last night, her wedding night, and all that had happened, good and bad. She worried that she didn't know her new husband—and that perhaps she would not have time to come to know him either. Had she made a mistake? Had she moved too hastily?

But she had come to find that unless one moved hastily in wartime the opportunity could be lost for ever.

When she ducked out of the tent she found herself in the midst of chaos. Soldiers were rushing around amid wagons being loaded and horses being saddled.

Another nurse ran past, and Catalina grabbed her arm. 'What is happening?' she cried.

'It is the push to Toulouse at last! The regiment's orders have come.'

'Already?' Catalina had known this day was

coming; it was why they had made camp here in the first place. But so very soon?

'The regiment is moving out today, that is all I know,' the nurse said. 'But we are to stay a few more days to make sure the wounded are seen to.'

She ran off again, and Catalina knew she had to find Jamie. She made her way through the maze of tents, many of which were being taken down, and passed by the tangle of people and horses. At last she glimpsed him, talking to Colonel Chambers. She started towards him, only to feel a hand on her arm, holding her back hard.

She glanced back to find Hugh Webster smiling at her. 'Mrs Moreno, I must talk to you....'

The strange, prickling feeling he always inspired in her shivered down her spine. She was not entirely sure why she disliked the man so much, but she did. She shook her head and said, 'Not now, Captain Webster. I must go.'

And she looked back to Jamie to see that he had glimpsed her too. He made his way to her side through the crowd, and his handsome face looked so very solemn.

'You are moving out today?' she said.

'I must ride out within the hour,' he answered.

He took her arm and led her around to the line of trees behind the camp, where they had so often walked together before. Grey clouds were gathering on the horizon to block out the sunlight, as if to echo her sudden feeling of dread.

'But where are you going?' she asked, holding on to his hand.

'I am not sure yet. But I will write to you soon, and tell you where to meet me.' Jamie's arms suddenly came around her, pulling her close, and she shut her eyes to memorise the way he felt, his scent, everything about him. About this moment. She felt everything rushing in on them, faster than she had expected. Jamie was leaving. And even if—when—he did come back, there would be so much for them to work on, to try and understand.

'Will you be careful?' she whispered.

'Of course. If you will as well.'

Catalina gave a choked laugh. 'I am not the one hurtling into battle.'

'We will be together again soon, I promise. You must not worry, no matter what you hear of what is happening.' Jamie sounded confident, as confident as the smile he gave her, but still Catalina was so unsure.

She nodded and tried to give him a smile in return. 'Yes, we must. You have promised to show me Castonbury.'

He kissed her hard, as if he couldn't bear to let her go even as she clung to him.

'Until we meet again, my Catalina,' he said with one more kiss. And then he let her go and he was gone.

And Catalina sank to her knees, unable to hold back her tears.

Chapter Three

Jamie stood on the muddy banks of the Bidasoa river and examined its rough currents as the rain that had been threatening to come down all morning now beat at his head. He wiped the drops from his eyes and tried to look across to the other side, but the storm was too thick and grey.

'What do you think, Señor Hatherton?' he heard Xavier Sanchez say.

He turned to face the Spaniard, who stood several safer feet back with the horses. Xavier was one of the Spanish agents working for the British government and had been Jamie's contact on many previous errands. He was usually a brave man, but today his dark eyes were cautious as he peered out at the river from under his sodden hat.

Jamie turned back to the water. His instructions

had been clear; he had to get to Toulouse before the regiment and rendezvous with their Spanish contacts. He had to cross the river to do that, just as the rest of the army would soon have to do, and time was of the essence.

And the sooner he finished this job, the sooner he would be able to return to Catalina…and the sooner they could start a real life together.

'We need to move closer to Toulouse as soon as possible,' Jamie said. 'And you must carry word back to camp of an "accident" so we can separate.'

'But the river, *señor*…'

'We are travelling light,' Jamie said. And he was a strong swimmer from long days on the lake at Castonbury with his siblings. 'I need to move today. You can follow on later, as we planned.'

Sanchez looked doubtful, but he nodded. 'I will follow with the horses soon, Señor Hatherton.'

Jamie stripped off his coat and boots and tucked them then into the saddlebags. He carefully waded into the water that rushed up over the banks. It was freezing cold, swollen by the rain, and his legs went numb as the currents swirled around them. When the water reached his waist, he took a breath and dived deep.

The cold closed over him like a thousand knives, but he pushed away the pain and kept swimming. He couldn't see anything around him, just swirls of grey and brown. He could only push towards where he knew the opposite bank lay. The deception of his accident had suddenly become all too real.

He was moving strongly, the only thought in his mind his goal. Suddenly a strong current jolted him like a blow to the midsection. It caught him and tossed him around, pushing him even as he fought against it. He felt himself being swept inexorably downstream, twisted and turned.

He struggled fiercely against the water, writhing in its powerful grip. Everything was turning grey and hazy as he couldn't surface for a breath.

Catalina's face was suddenly clear in his mind, her smile, her dark eyes. He had to fight this, to get back to her.

Something suddenly brushed past his hand, and he reached out to grab on to it. It was the root of a tree on the bank, sticking out into the river. He held on to its rough, delicate-seeming strength even as the water worked to claim him. He pulled himself up and sucked in a deep breath of precious air.

But the respite was not to last. Something hard and heavy, borne on the current, slammed into his body. He fell back down into the deep water and his head landed on something sharp. As if from a distance, he heard a sickening crack. There was a piercing pain—and everything went dark as the river closed over him.

'Catalina! Quick, over here. I need your help.'

Catalina spun around from the bandage she was tying off on a wounded arm to see one of the other nurses and the English doctor labouring over another patient. She gave her own soldier one more smile and hurried to help them.

The hospital tent had been chaos all day. The push to Toulouse was beginning in earnest, with different regiments pouring through and leaving their wounded to be seen to. Most of them moved on after, in a hurry to join with the main forces, but the people who were left had to tend to the sick and arrange for their transportation onwards as the French were in quick pursuit. The rain that had been pouring down steadily only added to the clamour, miring everyone in mud and damp. Gunfire was constantly heard in the distance.

Catalina had hardly slept or eaten since Jamie left. She had no time to think of such things as she ran from task to task, always hearing those explosions in the distance, rivalling the thunder. The world had shrunk to only that noise, and emergency after emergency.

But she couldn't cease worrying about Jamie. Was he well? Was he safe? What dangerous task was he embroiled in? Reports of flooding at the Bidasoa made her even more concerned. She had received no message from him yet.

All she could do was keep working, keep helping everyone she could.

'Soon,' she whispered as she rinsed her hands in a basin. Jamie would be back soon.

As she dried her hands, she glimpsed the sapphire ring glinting on her finger. It was always with her, reminding her of hopes and dreams that felt so very fragile now.

She pushed away her worries and went to help with the new patient. Once he was seen to, there was another and then another. The day had grown very late by the time she was able to duck out of the hot, stuffy tent for a breath of fresh air.

The rain had ceased for the moment, though the sound of gunfire seemed even closer. Catalina found a quiet spot by a tree just outside camp where she could be alone just for an instant. She tilted her head back to stare at the dark grey sky and let the cool breeze wash over her.

She thought about what Jamie had said about his home, about the beauty and peace of it. She feared she would get lost in its grandeur, but she did long for something pretty, something quiet. Someplace where she could walk with Jamie, hand in hand, the two of them in the fresh English spring.

'Mrs Moreno, what a surprise,' someone said suddenly, shattering her reverie. 'I so seldom see you alone.'

Catalina whirled around to see Hugh Webster smiling at her. The man seemed friendly, but somehow she always felt so uncomfortable when he was around her. He was friends with Colonel Chambers and had thus been assigned to help pack up the regiment and follow them on later while most of the men pushed ahead in greater danger. She had been working so hard she had hardly seen him, but here he was, right in front of her, as if he had been watching for her to be alone.

And he was standing much too close to her.

'We all have many tasks these days, Captain Webster,' she answered.

'True. Yet you have always seemed to have the time to speak to Hatherton.'

Catalina was puzzled by the bitter note in the man's voice. He smiled at her, but his eyes were hard. 'Lord Hatherton and I are friends.'

'Indeed? I wish you would be *my* friend, Mrs Moreno—Catalina. I am sure we could benefit each other a great deal.'

He took a step closer, until his arm brushed hers and she could smell the scent of his body. Catalina stumbled back until she felt the rough bark of the tree.

'Benefit each other?' she stammered.

'Of course, my dear. You must have seen how I admire you. It can be very lonely here, can it not? Especially for a woman in your…situation.'

'I don't know what you mean,' Catalina managed to say, shocked and starting to be frightened.

She spun around to hurry away, but suddenly his hand closed hard on her arm and dragged her back.

'Oh, I think you *do* know what I mean,' he said roughly. His arms came around her like a vice and his mouth swooped down on hers, open and hungry.

Catalina was engulfed in a cold panic. It felt as if prison walls were squeezing in on her, and nausea choked her. Webster's kiss was nothing like Jamie's; it didn't even deserve the same name. She fought against him, but he was too strong and held her fast. One of his hands closed on her breast through her muslin gown and he pinched painfully at her nipple.

Catalina screamed against his mouth and felt him laugh. That sound infuriated her. She managed to wriggle enough room between them to bring her knee up and slam it between his legs. When he shouted, she bit down on his lip and tasted coppery blood.

As he fell to the ground, she wrenched away and ran. She heard him scream out behind her. 'Whore!' he called. 'Hatherton's whore. You'll be sorry for this.'

'I am his wife!' Catalina screamed. 'Not his whore, you dirty *cochino*.'

She kept running, still half blind with fear. At first she didn't know what a sudden booming noise was, she was so disoriented. But as she stumbled and half fell to her knees, she saw a flaring flash of flame arc over the sky and heard cries.

The camp was being directly shelled.

As she watched, horrorstruck, more explosions went off around the camp amid shouts and screams. Fires were flaring up. She pushed herself up and ran towards the nearest tent. A shell exploded not far away, making her ears ring, but she kept going. She had to help if she could.

She glimpsed a figure lying on the ground, horribly still. It was the nurse she had worked with over the patient earlier. Catalina knelt down next to her, but she quickly saw it was too late to help her at all.

Suddenly a hand grabbed her arm and dragged her to her feet.

'Run, Catalina!' the man shouted. 'We must find shelter now.'

Catalina turned her head and saw it was the

English doctor, leading a couple of the more mobile wounded soldiers from the burning camp.

'But the others...' she gasped.

'Those who could flee have already gone,' the doctor answered. 'I fear the chaplain has been killed. The French are close in their pursuit. We must go, *now*.'

Catalina ran with him back towards the trees, where they found a hiding place in the shadows, their heads down as the shells flew overhead and they prayed the French armies wouldn't find them. Once darkness gave them cover, they fled towards the village with the few other survivors.

Only the next morning, as they stumbled out onto the road to Seville, did she see to her horror that she had lost her precious sapphire ring....

'So you are alive.'

Jamie opened his eyes to find a man standing over him, his features a blur from the light that streamed from the windows behind him. It was the first time he had heard anyone speak in that crisp English accent in days, ever since Sanchez had pulled him out of the river and slung him over the horse to find a hospital. They had ended in this house in a small village.

At first Jamie had been in such a strange dream state he was able to remember nothing at all. Only snatches of hazy memories, like a summer's day in the Castonbury gardens and Catalina's hand in his as they walked down the aisle. Gradually things became clearer, the pain sharper, and he cursed his damnable weakness. He had to finish what he had set out to do and get back to Catalina.

The man stepped back, and Jamie saw it was Lord Cawley, who had been his contact for secret work in Spain, the man who had sent him the letter requesting his assistance in the matter with the royal family.

There was surely only one thing he would be doing there.

Jamie gave a humourless laugh and pushed himself up against the pillows. 'I hadn't thought to see you so soon, Cawley.'

'No? Why not? I came at once when Sanchez sent word you were injured. We feared you might have died.'

'And thus you would get no more work out of me?'

'You have been one of our best operatives, Hatherton,' Cawley said. He pulled up a straight-backed wooden chair and sat down. His thin, lined face looked even harsher than usual. 'These are perilous days. After the French are gone, we have to be sure Spain is once again a friendly ally for England. It is of vital importance.'

'And you think King Ferdinand is the answer to that,' Jamie said drily.

'It is. He is not the finest choice, we admit, but he is the best option for now. Europe must have stability once Napoleon is gone. You are the best choice for such a vital and delicate operation.'

'I fear I can no longer be of help to you,' Jamie said.

'No?' Cawley tapped his fingers on the arm of the chair, watching Jamie steadily. 'That is unfortunate. The timing could not be better for our scheme.'

'What do you mean?'

'I mean that it is already rumoured you died in the river, tragically swept away. You could go undercover with no one the wiser.' Cawley gestured around the quiet little white room. 'No one knows where you are. And sadly your camp was destroyed by the French in the chaos after you departed.'

Jamie sat up straight, his muscles tense with alarm, his mind buzzing. Surely he had not just heard the man's words right. 'The camp was destroyed?'

'Yes. You have not been told? Such a tragedy. So many lives lost, including the wounded and even women.' Cawley reached inside his coat and withdrew a small scrap of blue-grey muslin. He unwrapped it to reveal a sapphire ring.

The gold was scratched and dirt was caught in the setting, but Jamie could see it was his mother's ring. The one he had slipped onto Catalina's finger. Wrapped in a torn shred of one of her work dresses.

'This was found in the camp ruins,' Cawley said. 'Yours, I think. It has your family motto engraved inside.'

He tossed it across the room and Jamie caught it. *Validus Superstes* was indeed engraved on the inside. Catalina had vowed she would never take it off after their wedding. If it was here, in Cawley's possession...

'You gave it to someone?' Cawley said quietly. 'I can't imagine you would have dropped it yourself.'

'A lady named Catalina Moreno,' Jamie answered, closing his fist around the ring as if that would bring her back to him. Even in that moment he could feel her slipping further and further away.

Cawley nodded. 'The Spanish nurse. One of the lost, I fear.'

Lost. Catalina was lost, lost, lost. Those words echoed hollowly in his head, yet still he could not quite grasp them. She was the most vivid person he had ever known—how could she simply be gone, just like that?

A sharp pain shot through him, a jolt of purest, hottest grief. Then a cold numbness as if ice was slowly creeping around his heart.

'Perhaps that is for the best,' Cawley said. 'Her brother was known to be a liberal, even though he has been long dead. She would only have stood in the way of what is best. And I would hate to see harm come to anyone in your family because you could not do your duty. I am sure you understand what I mean.'

Harm come to anyone in your family. Of course

he knew what the man meant; it was a veiled threat pure and simple. Jamie tightened his hand on the ring until the edges of the stone cut into his flesh. He closed his eyes and let that ice cover him. It had to be better than the burn of grief, of knowing he would never see Catalina again and that he had not been there to save her when she needed him.

Yes—he had failed Catalina. And his family would be better off without him as well. Had he not run off and left them because he was unsure he could assume the responsibilities of a dukedom? Had he not already failed in his duty? At least he could protect them now by doing this task. And if he was lucky he would not return from it.

As if he sensed Jamie's cold fury, Cawley rose from his chair and turned towards the door. 'Everyone already believes you dead, Hatherton. It makes you the perfect one for this job. And when it's over you can return to your family, knowing the service you did for your country. Send me word of your decision tomorrow.'

Then Jamie was alone. He closed his eyes and held on to the ring as if it was the last tether anchoring him to the real world. The last connection to his foolish dreams. Catalina was gone, and Cawley was right—it hardly mattered what happened to him now.

But first he had to do something for himself.

Chapter Four

It looked like the landscape of another world entirely, not a place where he had once lived and worked, fought and loved. It was a place he had never seen before except in nightmares.

Jamie felt strangely numb, remote from his surroundings as he climbed stiffly down from his horse and studied the scorched patch of earth where the camp once stood. The hot sun beat down from a clear, mercilessly blue sky onto the baked, cracked dust, but Jamie didn't even feel it. He was vaguely aware of Xavier Sanchez, sitting on his own horse several feet away and watching the scene warily, but Jamie felt like the only living being left for miles around.

Maybe the only living being left on the planet.

There were no sounds, no birds singing or wind

sweeping through the trees. Once this place had been filled with voices, laughter, the cries of the injured, the barked orders of a military operation. The ghosts of such sounds in his mind made the silence even heavier.

Jamie tilted back his head to stare up into the sky. He could smell the dusty scent of the air, the faint, acrid remains of fire. The echoes of the violence that had happened here.

And Catalina had been caught in it. His numbness was shattered by a spasm of pure, raw pain at the thought of what must have happened here. The fear and panic, the sense of being trapped amid fire and ruin with nowhere to run. No one to help her, because he had gone.

'Catalina,' he whispered, his heart shattered at the thought of her being afraid. Had she thought of him in that moment, just as he had pictured only her face when he was sure he was drowning? Had she called out his name?

Jamie walked slowly across the blasted, blackened patch of earth, not seeing it how it was now, abandoned and ruined, but how it was that day he first saw Catalina. Her smile, her face like a beautiful, exotic flower, a haven of peace and loveliness in a mad world. She had given him something he had never known before—stillness, a place to belong. She had made him think of things he had never dared to before, like a future, a home. With her, he had imagined even the grand halls of Castonbury could be that home, if she was there.

And then in only a moment that was all gone.

He remembered her hurt, pale face when she found out about the nature of his secret work. The doubts that lingered in her eyes when they parted. He had foolishly imagined he would have time to make all that right later, to make everything up to her.

Jamie reached up and pressed his hand over the ring he wore on a chain around his neck under his shirt, against his heart. Cawley had said this ring, Catalina's ring, had been found here among the dead. Yet some stubborn hope had clung to Jamie—what if she had somehow miraculously got away?

Cawley had said a farmer found the ring, and that was what had brought Jamie here. He had discovered the name of the farmer and come back to the camp in the wild, far-fetched notion that he could find this man and make him tell more details of the day when the camp was destroyed. If he knew more, maybe he could find Catalina's body and put her properly to rest.

Or he might find *her*. At night, in his fever dreams when he was ill, he saw just such a thing. Catalina, alive again, smiling at him, holding out her arms to him. Telling him it had all been a terrible mistake.

But as he looked at the darkened earth, he saw just how wild a hope that was. Surely no one had survived such an onslaught.

He climbed to the top of a steep slope into which the backside of the camp had been built. It led down to the river on the other side, and to fields beyond. They, too, were deserted, everyone having fled before the advancing armies. But Jamie glimpsed one tiny spot of life, an old woman walking by the river, swathed in shawls even in the hot day. She was checking fishing nets laid out in the river.

Jamie made his way slowly down the other side of the hill, careful to make sure the woman saw him approach so he would not frighten her. She didn't run away, but went very still, her eyes dark and wary in her sunken, wrinkled face.

'*Señora*, I only came to ask a few questions here,' Jamie said in Spanish.

The woman slowly nodded, and he asked her about the destruction of the camp. She didn't know much; she had been staying with her daughter in another village, and had only returned to her home here with her son after the armies had gone.

'What do you seek here, young man?' she asked. 'There is nothing left, not for anyone.'

'I want to find out what happened to my wife,' Jamie answered honestly. 'She was a nurse at the English camp here. I was told a farmer saw what happened, and found her wedding ring.'

The woman nodded, her face softening at his stark words. 'Come with me,' she said. 'Perhaps my son can help. He was here that day, I am sure he's the one you're looking for.'

She led him over a low, crumbling stone wall and through a blasted field. A man was working there, bent and careworn as he tried to eke out some kind of meal from the ruined ground. Even though the woman said he was her son, he looked as old as she did. But his eyes also turned kind when the woman explained why Jamie was there.

'I did see the camp after the French left,' he said, leaning on his rake with a haunted look in his eyes. 'I wanted to see if I could help, but there was nothing left to do but bury the dead.'

Jamie took out Catalina's ring and showed it to him. 'Were you the one who found this?'

The man nodded, tears in his eyes. 'I found it in the dust, near a woman's body. It had been trampled down, half buried.'

Jamie swallowed hard at the stark words. Catalina's ring trampled, destroyed. 'This woman— did she have dark hair? Not very tall?'

'*Sí*, she looked Spanish, but her skin was pale with freckles on the nose. And she wore a nurse's apron.'

Jamie closed his fist around the ring. 'And you gave this back to the English? That was very generous of you, considering you could have sold it.'

The man shrugged. 'I wouldn't want to bring curses onto my family. What if the woman's spirit attached to the ring?'

Jamie stared down at the sapphire, almost wishing that he, too, could believe in curses. That Catalina could stay with him through her ring. 'What happened to the woman's body?'

The man turned away silently, and led Jamie over the field to an empty meadow that lay just beyond. There the dirt was piled in a long, heaped-up mound, with a line of roughly hewn crosses.

'They were all buried here,' the man said. 'She is down there at that end. I laid her there myself.'

Jamie moved slowly towards the grave. The world slowed to a blur around him, and he felt so numb again, old, remote from everything. All he could see was that patch of earth.

He knelt down and for a moment grief pressed in all around him and he was utterly alone. Catalina was buried here; he could feel it. His family was far away, and in this, the most profound moment of his life, he was alone.

'I am so sorry, Catalina,' he said. Sorry he had not been there for her; sorry he could not have been what she needed him to be. Sorry he had ever hurt her at all.

He tilted back his head and stared up into the sky, feeling so very empty. He had to finish his task here in Spain, no matter how distasteful it was. He had to do it for his family.

But he feared he himself would never feel anything again.

* * *

Catalina leaned against the railing of the ship and peered through the thick, wet grey mist at the slowly approaching shoreline.

England. She was in England at last. And she didn't notice the sharp, cold wind that tore at her hat or the noise and activity on the deck behind her. She could only think about how close her destination was, after weeks of weary travel—and of how different this arrival was from how she had once so briefly pictured it. How she had once dreamed it might be, with Jamie by her side, taking her home with him.

She curled her gloved hand into a tight fist. The brief, dizzying days of her romance and marriage seemed so far away now, a vision clouded by months of trying to survive as she travelled across war-torn Spain. Yet still she could see Jamie's face so clearly in her mind, could hear his voice calling her name and feel his hand on hers.

At night she lay awake, unable to sleep as she remembered him. She was plagued by so many thoughts, so many questions she was sure could never be answered now that he was gone. What had really happened to him? Who had gone on to do his mission of restoring the Spanish king?

Had he thought of her there at the end? Had he loved her? Had their time together brought him any peace at all?

She did hope so. And she hoped that one day her heart would not feel so shattered and lonely whenever she thought of him.

The shore was looming closer with every moment, dark and shadowed in the rain but unmistakably green, just as she had pictured England when Jamie told her about his homeland. Somewhere out there was his home, Castonbury, and his family, mourning him as she was.

'Mrs Moreno! There you are,' she heard her employer, Mrs Burnes, say. Catalina turned to see the lady emerging from below decks, bundled in shawls and scarves, her face pale under her fashionable bonnet.

Catalina smiled and hurried to her side. She liked Mrs Burnes, and considered herself fortunate to have the job of her companion on the voyage home to England. Her husband, General Burnes, had sent her away from Spain for the sake of her health and safety. Mrs Burnes was rather sickly and sometimes quite demanding, but she was not mean as Mrs Chambers had often been to poor Alicia Walters. She enjoyed hearing Catalina read to her to distract her from the rough seas, and the days passed well enough on the voyage.

It was the nights, when she was alone with no duties to perform, that filled Catalina with thoughts of Jamie.

She helped Mrs Burnes onto a deckchair and tucked the shawls closer around her. 'We are almost there now, Mrs Burnes. Land at last.'

'Thank heavens for that! I could never bear another sea voyage,' Mrs Burnes said. 'Once my dear general is home, I shall insist we never leave again.'

Catalina laughed. 'I can definitely agree to that, Mrs Burnes. The sea is not so agreeable as land.'

'Oh, but surely you will want to return to Spain one day, Mrs Moreno. When things are settled there.'

Catalina shook her head. 'This will be my home now.' She couldn't go back to Spain, not with the king returning. Not with all the memories lurking there.

'Well, I hope you will like England, then. It's

very different from Spain, but there are interesting sights and people to be found here as well, if one only looks.' Mrs Burnes chattered on as the ship lumbered towards shore, telling Catalina about all her friends in London she hoped to see again and the country house she wanted to buy as soon as her husband returned so they could retire there together.

'…it is very near Castonbury Park, the seat of the Duke of Rothermere,' Mrs Burnes said.

The words caught Catalina's attention. 'Castonbury?' she said, and all the tales Jamie had told her of his home came flooding back to her.

'Oh, yes. Have you heard of the house? It is one of the loveliest in all England, and surely one of the grandest. I toured it once as a girl, and I still remember the great marble columns and the lovely frescoes on the ceilings! Just what a Roman emperor's palace must have been like, I imagine. I even caught a glimpse of the duchess, who was just going out for a ride. She was so very beautiful and elegant, just what an English duchess ought to be.' Mrs Burnes sighed. 'That is the sort of thing I will be happy to return to, something so *English*.'

Catalina almost laughed. Once, she might have been mistress of that place, a new duchess. Yet all she had wanted was Jamie, Jamie who turned out to be a dream creation of her own romantic heart.

But she still almost wished she could see the house just once. See it, and imagine Jamie was somehow still with her there...

Chapter Five

England, two years later

Jamie stared out of the carriage window as the hedgerows rolled by, a blur of bright green in the English summer sunshine. It could be anywhere in England, any country lane, yet he knew it could only be one place. *Home.* So familiar, like it was a very part of his blood and bones, and yet so very alien. So different from the Spanish landscape he had lived with for so long.

His leg ached after the long days of travel, and he shifted it across the cramped confines of the hired carriage. It was so strange that this land seemed to have remained over the years so unchanged when he was a different person. All he had seen and done. All the mistakes he had made.

He couldn't imagine what they would say when he reached Castonbury, or what he would find there.

Jamie closed his eyes wearily and ran his hand over his jaw. He could feel the rough growth of a couple days' beard over the slashing arc of his scar. Yes, he *was* different now, not the reckless young man who had dashed off in search of adventure all those years ago. The scars were only the outward show of his darkened soul. He had a sudden image of his family fleeing before him, of his father slamming the doors in his face.

And he would be within his rights to do so. Jamie was sure he had failed as a son and brother, just as he had failed as a husband. He had left his family to financial hardship and mourning; he had lost Catalina and betrayed her ideals.

Jamie cracked his walking stick against the floor, as if the violent movement could erase Catalina's face from his mind. But she was still there, as she always was, reminding him of what he had lost. The sapphire ring he wore on a chain around his neck.

He couldn't save Catalina now, she was beyond him. But he *could* do his duty to his family now and make up for all his mistakes. All his life he had secretly fought against the idea of being the duke, of having the power and the responsibility in his hands. But surely he was ready now.

He had to be. He had to see to solving his family's financial troubles, and disposing of this imposter trying to claim the dukedom for a child that wasn't his.

The carriage lurched as it swayed around a sharp turn in the lane, and Jamie looked up to find the ornate iron gates of Castonbury before him. They stood open, as if to welcome him home, the prodigal son. He remembered running out of them and down the lane, chased by his siblings—Kate, Phaedra, Giles, Harry and poor lost Edward.

The gardens beyond the gate were not quite as he remembered. The flower beds were not as impeccably tended as they once were, the vast, rolling lawns not as green and velvety, and some of the statues and marble benches were chipped and overturned. But financial solvency would soon fix all of that and set it to its rightful splendour.

And just ahead was Castonbury, gleaming white in the sunshine, its staircase twining around to sweep up to the pillared portico built to impress every guest who approached.

As the carriage slowed along the curve of the drive, with the grand portico just before them hung with fresh beribboned garlands, Jamie looked up at the windows glowing like diamonds in the light. One of them was open, pale curtains fluttering in the breeze, and he suddenly pictured all the eyes that could be peering out through that old glass. Eyes that would watch him lurch from the carriage and limp up the steps of his home.

He lowered the carriage window and called out, 'Around to the back, I think.'

The hired coachman shrugged and turned the horses around the lane to follow the side of the house. In the distance he could see a paddock with new horses.

The carriage finally drew to a halt outside the servants' entrance. Jamie pushed the door open and lowered himself to the gravelled drive, leaning on his walking stick. For an instant, the sun was in his eyes and he peered up at the shadow of the house as the warm breeze swept up from the kitchen gardens. It even *smelled* the same, of fresh, green grass, herbs from the garden, the scent of baking bread that rolled out from the kitchens all the time.

Jamie closed his eyes and thought of how many times he had stolen sweets from the kitchens with his brothers and sisters and gone running out of those doors and down the path to the lake. How they had shouted to one another and laughed and teased, as if there was no other time but that moment, no one in the world but themselves. Giles, Harry, Edward, Kate and Phaedra.

Edward. A spasm of raw pain went over him as he thought of how he would never see Edward again. His brother was gone, lost at Waterloo, and Jamie hadn't been at Castonbury with the others to mourn him.

'I am here now,' he said. Even though Castonbury felt like a dream, like something completely unreal, he *was* there. And he had work to do.

The door to the kitchen was half open, and Jamie pushed his way through it into the corridor. The hallway was deserted, but he could hear the echo of voices and the clatter of china from the warren of rooms beyond. He followed the sound, the tap of his boots and stick hollow on the flagstone floor.

'No, not there!' he heard the housekeeper, Mrs Stratton, say sternly. 'Those must be put on ice immediately, and the flowers should be put there to be arranged. This wedding must be *perfect*, we have waited for it so long.'

A wedding—of course. That would explain the garlands out front and the hectic air here in the servants' hall, the haze of excitement that seemed to hang over everything. Jamie remembered Harry saying their brother Giles was set to marry Lily Seagrove after a long engagement, but he hadn't said when it was to be. If Jamie had known when it was, he might have stayed away until it was all over.

Weddings were not his favourite things. Not since that quiet little chapel in Spain.

He glanced back at the open door and the ray of sunlight that seemed to beckon him to freedom, but it was too late. A maidservant suddenly came scurrying out of the servants' corridor, her arms full of roses and lilies bound up in paper. Jamie stepped back, but she collided with him anyway and the flowers fell in a scatter of pink and white over the floor.

'Oh, laws, but you scared me!' she cried. 'I didn't half expect anyone to be there.'

'I am so very sorry,' Jamie said ruefully. What a beginning he was making of his homecoming! 'Here, let me help you.'

He started to kneel down to gather the flowers, but the girl let out another shriek. 'Are you a ghost?' she said, and Jamie looked up to see that she had covered her face with her hands.

'I—no,' Jamie said, completely bemused. 'Sometimes I feel rather like one, but I am told I'm still alive.'

'You look like the one in that painting that's all draped in black and such,' the girl sobbed. She peeked between her hands and shook her head. 'I swear that's you!'

His portrait was hung in black? Before Jamie could ask the girl about it, or tell her to pinch him to show her he was alive, he heard Mrs Stratton call, 'Mary! What are you doing making so much noise out there?'

Jamie heard the rustle of fabric and looked up to find the housekeeper standing in the doorway. She looked so much as she had on those long-ago days of childhood wildness, her blonde hair mixed with silver, her blue eyes kind. She stared at him with her mouth open, a rare instance of discomposure from the woman who had run Castonbury with such efficiency for so long.

'I am sorry, Mrs Stratton,' he said. 'I'm afraid I startled her.'

'L-Lord Hatherton?' she whispered. 'Is it really you?'

'It is me,' Jamie said. He could think of nothing else to say, nothing that could smooth his homecoming. 'I'm sorry to have arrived at such an inconvenient time. I understand a wedding is imminent.'

Mrs Stratton shook her head, her eyes bright. 'We thought never to see you again, my lord. Any moment you arrived would be...' She shook her head again and seemed to compose herself. 'Welcome back to Castonbury, my lord.'

'Thank you, Mrs Stratton. It's...' Strange? Difficult? Painful? '...good to be back.'

Mrs Stratton reached down for the maid's arm and pulled her to her feet. 'Stop that caterwauling at once, girl. It is only Lord Hatherton. You need to gather those flowers immediately and see that they get to Ellen for arranging. They need to be in the drawing room well before tonight's dinner party.'

Mary gave a squeak and hurriedly scooped up the flowers before she ran off.

'A dinner party?' Jamie said in alarm.

'Merely a small dinner, my lord,' Mrs Stratton said. 'The family is upstairs getting dressed after an afternoon in the gardens. Your father will probably not attend, I think.'

Jamie remembered what Harry had said about their father's health, that he seldom left his rooms these days. 'Is he unwell today?'

'No, it has been rather a good day for the duke, my lord. He is excited about the wedding, as we all are. But he does have his good times and his bad times.' Mrs Stratton gave him a smile. 'I am sure seeing you will make this the best of days.'

Another twinge of guilt touched Jamie. 'I hope I can be of help now that I am home, Mrs Stratton. I will try to stay out of the way for the wedding.'

'Nonsense, my lord! You could never be in the way. You were always the best behaved of all the Montague children.'

Jamie laughed wryly, remembering all his childhood pranks. 'I fear you are too kind to me.'

'Not at all.' Mrs Stratton's eyes were suspiciously bright again, but she shook her head and said, 'Shall I take you to the duke, then, my lord? He likes to have a small brandy and some cakes at this hour. It livens up his evening a bit.'

Brandy and cakes? It seemed like such a small world for the man he remembered as larger than life. 'Thank you, Mrs Stratton. I would appreciate that.'

As Jamie followed the housekeeper through the kitchens, he saw how truly busy everyone was. The maids and footmen dashed around, bearing gowns and cravats to be pressed, flowers to be arranged and trays of refreshments. The clatter of pots and pans and silver was in the air, which smelled of roasting chicken and cinnamon spices. But as he passed, they all froze in their paths to stare. When he nodded to them, they hurriedly curtsied and bowed and scurried on their errands.

Did they think he was a ghost as well? A spectre haunting the party.

He followed Mrs Stratton up the winding stairs, past more maids carrying flowers, and through the green baize doors that divided the warm, noisy servants' realm from the outer world of Castonbury.

But even here everything was noise and movement, splashes of colour amid the shadows. Vases of flowers stood against the dark walls and garlands were twined along the staircase banisters. Jamie couldn't remember so much colour in the house since his mother, with her love of parties, had died so long ago. It felt almost like the house was coming awake again after a long sleep.

If only it could thaw his own soul.

'How is your son faring, Mrs Stratton?' he asked as they turned down a long, narrow gallery lined with portraits in their old, heavily gilded frames. The first duke who had once been an earl, his grandfather, his uncle, his mother with Jamie in his infant days clinging to her skirts. All as familiar to him as his own face in the mirror.

Yet even they seemed very far away, not a real part of him at all.

'Adam?' Mrs Stratton said. A smile touched her lined face. 'He is quite well, my lord. He is married now, you know, to Amber Hall from the village. They are living in Lancashire where he has his business concerns. I hope to join them there after the wedding.' She did not mention the fact that had recently come to light, that Amber had turned out to be their illegitimate half-sister.

'You are leaving Castonbury?' Jamie asked in surprise. 'The house will not be the same without you.' And it truly would not. Mrs Stratton had been a part of Castonbury as long as he could remember.

'I am too old to do a worthy job here much longer, my lord,' Mrs Stratton said with a laugh. 'But I am training Rose, one of the upstairs maids who has been here a while, to take over as housekeeper. It will be nice to be closer to my son.'

'I hope that he is happy in his marriage,' Jamie said, a vision of Catalina in her lace veil flashing through his mind. Hopefully Adam and Amber would enjoy a long and happy life together, the kind he had hoped to have with Catalina.

'Indeed he is. We have all hoped...' Mrs Stratton suddenly broke off and gave him an odd glance, her smile flickering into a frown.

Jamie was sure she wanted to ask about his own supposed 'marriage', and he was reminded of all the strange things that must have happened at Castonbury while he was gone. And of all he still had to do.

Which probably included finding a future duchess to marry. He shook his head. There was enough to do without torturing himself with that now.

At the end of the gallery, Mrs Stratton turned not towards his father's grand suite of ducal chambers but to another, narrower corridor.

She seemed to see his surprise for she gave him a small smile. 'Your father prefers to spend his days in a small sitting room he set up for himself when Lord Edward died. It's quieter on this side of the house.'

'I see,' Jamie said, though in truth he did not. He still had a lot of things to relearn here.

'His health has been so much improved since Lord Harry returned from Spain,' Mrs Stratton said. 'I believe he is even looking forward to the wedding! But I must tell you, my lord, that the doctors say he should be kept as calm as possible.'

Jamie almost laughed aloud at the thought that anyone could keep his father 'calm' when he did not wish to be. But he merely nodded as Mrs Stratton knocked at a door.

'Your Grace?' she called softly. 'You have a visitor.'

'Not another cursed visitor!' a hoarse voice answered, muffled by the thick wood of the door. 'This place is full of them.'

Mrs Stratton just opened the door and stepped inside. Jamie followed her, his hand curled hard around the head of his stick. The room was dim, the only light from a crackling fire that burned in the grate despite the warm day outside. The draperies were drawn over the windows, and a large, overstuffed armchair was drawn close to the hearth.

At first Jamie thought the housekeeper had brought him to the wrong room and a stranger sat before him. An elderly stranger, thin and spare compared to his robust, hearty father, the man who had ridden hell for leather with the local hunt and whose voice could thunder down the vast corridors of Castonbury. The man who sat before the fire had grey hair and a thick shawl wrapped around his shoulders. The air was heavy and stifling.

'You gave orders that you wanted to see *this* visitor right away, Your Grace,' Mrs Stratton said.

She glanced at Jamie and gave him a small, encouraging smile before she left.

'I did no such…' The man twisted around in his chair, and a pair of blue-grey eyes—Montague eyes—looked at Jamie from the gloom. It *was* his father, after all, grown old while he had been gone.

'James,' his father whispered. He braced his age-spotted hands on the chair's arms and tried to push himself to his feet, but he fell back to the cushions. 'James, is it you? Is it?'

Jamie hurried forward as fast as his cursed leg would let him. He caught his father on his second attempt to rise and held him upright. 'Yes, Father,' he answered. 'It is me. Past time I came home, eh?'

To his shock, the duke—a man who had seldom had time for his children when he was so busy with his duties and his sporting life—caught Jamie's shoulders in his thin hands and dragged him closer.

'James, James,' he whispered. 'Harry did say—but I didn't dare think it was true.'

Bewildered, Jamie patted his father's shoulder. *What a sorry pair we are*, he thought wryly.

A duke and a marquis, an old man and a cripple with their house falling down around them.

'Where have you been?' the duke said.

'Here, Father, sit down and I will tell you what I can.' Jamie helped his father back down to the chair. He quickly poured them each a measure of brandy from the tray on the sideboard by the wall and sat down across from his father to tell of his adventures in Spain.

'I'm sorry for everything, Father,' he said. He gulped down half the glass, relishing the bite of the brandy down his throat. 'It's not at all adequate, I know, but I do mean it.'

'You are here now—that's all that matters, James.' The duke took a trembling sip of his own drink. 'Harry says you had important work in Spain.'

Jamie told him as briefly as possible what had happened in Spain, or at least the part of the tale he *could* tell. Catalina was his alone, and she always would be. His secret. His wife.

The duke shook his head as Jamie finished his story. 'And while you were there you did *not* marry that woman. That is what Harry said. The child—the child is not yours. Ours.'

For an instant, Jamie thought his father meant Catalina. Then he remembered—Alicia Walters. He had turned over his few memories of her on his voyage home and tried to decide what to do. It was such a strange tale, and one that looked to get even stranger before it was ended. Even when the prodigal came home trouble followed.

But Harry had said their father had grown fond of the child, which meant Jamie had to go carefully. 'No, Father,' he answered gently. 'I did not marry her or father any child with her.'

'That harlot!' his father roared with a flare of his old temper. He pounded his fist on the arm of the chair. 'I knew it could not be, that you would not marry like that. She has made bloody fools of us all. She should hang for what she did! Bringing that child here…'

'Father,' Jamie said, in the quiet but firm voice that had worked to calm down so many people in Spain when it had been a matter of life and death. He had learned that desperate people did desperate things—and what Alicia had done reeked of desperation. He had to learn what had driven her to this, which would be hard enough without his family shouting for blood.

'Father,' he went on quietly. 'We don't want to see a woman hanged for this when it's better to be discreet. Think of the scandal. Have the Montagues not already given our neighbours enough to talk about?'

His father gave a loud, derisive snort, but Jamie saw that he did settle back into his chair and some of the red faded from his sunken cheeks. 'We have been embroiled in our share of scandal lately, I admit. Your brothers and sisters have chosen such odd matches.'

'Then let me take care of this. Surely I have the right to find out why someone would use my name this way.'

'Of course you do, James.'

Jamie sat back in his chair and drank down the last of his brandy as he looked into the fire. The flames had died down to mere sparking flickers amid the ash, reminding him of the smouldering ruins of the camp in Spain. The sapphire ring on the chain around his neck weighed heavily against his chest, and he thought again of the fleeting joys of life, the unknowability of other people.

He would never trust like that again.

'I learned a great deal in Spain, Father,' he said.

'And one thing I learned is that it's always better to find out all one can about one's enemies and then eliminate them quietly, with no fuss or mess. Leave as little as possible to clean up after.'

He felt his father watching him, and Jamie glanced up to find something he had never seen before flicker over the duke's face—uncertainty.

'What *did* you do in Spain, James?' he asked quietly.

Jamie shook his head. 'Spain is in the past, Father.' And it had to stay there, buried with Catalina. 'You have borne the burden of my absence for much too long. Let me take care of things now. I will deal with Alicia and any allies she might have, and I will also go to London as soon as possible and see about the money. You needn't worry any longer.'

His father nodded wearily, and in that one gesture Jamie could see how much things had truly changed at Castonbury. In years past, his father would never have relinquished the reins of the estate and the family to anyone, especially not one of his children.

'It is good to have you back, James,' the duke said.

Jamie rose to his feet and set aside his empty

glass. After a moment's hesitation, he laid his hand on his father's shoulder. 'It is good to be back. It's a new day here at Castonbury, Father, I promise. Giles is marrying now, and we should all be happy.' If only he could believe those words himself. If he could only be happy, as he had been for that one moment in the Spanish chapel.

But that was gone. Castonbury was all there was now.

His father nodded. 'He is not the only one who needs to be married, you know.'

'Father…'

'You know I am right, James,' the duke said with a trace of his old obstinacy. 'You have come back to take charge, and that is all well and good. But the first duty of a duke is to provide an heir. Since it is not little Crispin…'

The duke's voice faltered, and Jamie remembered how Harry had said their father had become so fond of Alicia's child. It almost made him wish the boy *was* his, so that duty would have been done.

He squeezed his father's shoulder and stepped back. 'There is time for all that later, Father. Let me see to more pressing matters first.'

'More pressing?' the duke sputtered. 'What could be more pressing than seeing to the future of Castonbury?'

'With Giles and Harry here and married, I hardly think the future is in doubt.'

'You have seen what happens when the heir is gone, James! No, *you* must marry and have children now.' The duke nodded firmly. 'I didn't want to see this wedding become so elaborate, but now I'm glad so many guests are coming. It will serve a most useful purpose.'

Jamie didn't like the sound of that. He gave his father a suspicious frown. 'What purpose is that?'

'To get you a wife! A *real* wife this time, a suitable one. A proper duchess.' His father nodded again. 'Your mother's cousin Lydia—you wouldn't remember her, she died ages ago, but she was a pretty thing who married a viscount. Her daughter is coming to the wedding. I hear she's a pretty girl herself, and just made her come-out last Season. She should do well enough.'

Jamie had to laugh. He had only been home a matter of hours and he was already being married off to some cousin he had never met. 'Father…'

'You will do your duty now, James!' his father shouted in an echo of his old self.

'Settle down, Father,' James said in his quiet voice. 'The girl isn't even here yet, so we have time before I must propose. We will see what happens.'

The duke nodded, as if he was at least slightly mollified. 'Very well. Just remember what I said. Duty!'

'Of course. Duty.'

'Now it grows late. You should go and dress for dinner, if you have any decent clothes after gallivanting around goodness knows where.' The duke reached for a bell on the little table beside his chair and rang it vigorously. After a moment, Mrs Stratton reappeared.

'Send Smithins to me,' the duke demanded. 'I want to dress for dinner.'

'Your Grace?' Mrs Stratton said. She gave Jamie a startled glance, and he shrugged. 'You haven't been downstairs to dinner in an age.'

'Then it's time that changed,' the duke said. 'My son is home now. Things here are going to be different. Starting with dinner.'

'I should go and change myself,' Jamie said,

not wanting to be there for what appeared to be shaping into an argument. 'If you will excuse me, Father.'

'Just remember what I said,' the duke shouted after Jamie as he left the room. 'Duty!'

Jamie shook his head. *Duty*—it had followed him all his life, like a ghostly spectre. He had fled from it to Spain, but still it was always with him. And now it was all he had. A consolation as well as a burden.

He knew his father was right. He *would* have to marry. But not yet. He had an imposter wife to dispatch and money matters to organise before he could start to restore Castonbury.

And he had another wife to forget.

Jamie made his way to the head of the grand staircase and peered down over the carved banisters to the entrance hall. It was as grand and forbidding as he remembered, with its carved columns soaring up to the Marble Hall above and the vast empty fireplaces. The classical statues in their niches stared out blindly.

It was quiet for the moment, all the servants off preparing for dinner and his family in their rooms dressing for dinner.

Jamie braced his palm on the banister and remembered how, long ago, the dignified silence of the house had been broken by him and his siblings as they dashed across the floor, shouting at one another, driving Mrs Stratton and the starchy, proper butler, Lumsden, to distraction. If his father had his way, soon enough Jamie's own children would be breaking free of the nursery to run through the house. But Jamie could not picture it. Not without Catalina.

Suddenly the solemn hush was broken when the front door burst open, letting in the light and wind of the dying day. A tall woman appeared there, the train of her dark green riding habit looped over her arm and a crop in her hand. Her boots rang out on the floor as she hurried towards the staircase, the sunset bright on her honey-coloured hair.

'Late again,' she muttered, dashing up the steps. 'Bother it all!'

Jamie laughed. Some things at Castonbury had clearly not changed, especially not his sister Phaedra. When she was with her horses everything else vanished for her.

She glanced up at the sound and a smile broke

across her face. She ran up the stairs and threw her arms around him, and for the first time he felt like he had truly come home.

'Jamie!' Phaedra cried. 'Oh, Jamie, is it really you? Are you truly back here with us at last?'

'I am,' he answered, holding her in his arms. His little sister, all grown up.

Suddenly she pulled back and smacked him hard on the arm. 'How could you have been gone from us all this time? I can't tell you how much we missed you, how much Castonbury has suffered.'

'I know,' Jamie said solemnly. 'And I am here to fix all that, I promise. You have worked alone here too long.'

'I have not been entirely alone. You know I have married.'

'Yes. A bloke named Basingstoke.'

'Bram,' Phaedra said, a soft smile replacing her frown. 'You will meet him at dinner. And tomorrow I am going to take you to look at the stables so we can talk about what is needed. I intend to make Castonbury the finest horse stud ever seen in England!' She linked arms with him and walked with him up the stairs, chattering away as she always had when they were children. 'You will be so proud of what we are doing here, Jamie! I can't tell you how glad I am you are home at last....'

Chapter Six

That had to be the place.

Jamie drew up his new curricle at the gate of the tiny, ramshackle cottage set at the edge of a wood several miles from Castonbury and far from any other houses or villages. The shutters were all drawn and no smoke curled from the chimney. With the overgrown gardens tangled around its peeling walls, it looked deserted. But his contact had assured him she was there.

When Jamie had gone looking for Alicia Walters, he had found it no easy task. She had fled from the Dower House at Castonbury as soon as Harry had returned from Spain. Her ruse had been discovered, and no one on the estate was sure where she had gone. His father, despite his blustering threats of hangings, hadn't chased after her, and his siblings were too relieved at learning that their brother was still alive to care. Only one person had seemed concerned about her, and that was the Castonbury estate manager, William Everett.

'I know what she did was terrible, my lord,' he had said to Jamie as they walked over the fields. 'But she must have been coerced in some way, I'm sure. She was too gentle to come up with such a scheme herself. I fear something amiss might have happened to her.'

Jamie had learned a great deal about reading people in Spain, about gauging the true thoughts and emotions they hid behind their words. Everett had worked for the Montagues for a long time and had a reputation for scrupulous honesty and openness. Jamie saw that his words were true—he did believe Alicia to be a good woman pressed in some way to do a bad thing. The man was concerned about her safety now.

And what was more, he cared about her. In his eyes Jamie could see the raw fear, the tenderness, when he said Alicia's name. The tentative spark of hope. He was afraid he himself had looked just like that when he first saw Catalina. Lovestruck. Foolish.

So Everett saw good in Alicia. But he didn't know where she had gone. Neither did anyone else on the estate or in Buxton, and most seemed to wish she would stay gone. But finding people who didn't wish to be found was something else Jamie had learned in Spain. When he went to London to settle the financial accounts, he had looked up some of his more disreputable contacts and got to work.

That work had led him here, to this deserted-looking cottage. It didn't look like a place where anyone could live, especially not a gentle lady with a small child, but perhaps that was its attraction. No one would think to look here, especially since it was actually close to Castonbury, plus the owner of the land had been abroad for a long time and would charge no rent. He wondered at the cunning mind that had discovered this clever hiding place, that had thought up this dastardly scheme in the first place

Jamie braced his leg against the seat and grimaced as he studied the silent house. He didn't need to use the stick to get about as much any more—the long walks over the estate to survey what needed to be done had helped with that. But the day in the curricle had made the scars stiffen.

'You just need to get on a horse again, get out in the hunting field,' Phaedra had said, sure that a good gallop could cure any ill. But he had laughed and told her that was still a long way in the future, and he had bought this curricle instead. Just one more thing he couldn't yet do that was expected of him as the heir.

Or maybe it was the knowledge of what he had to do now that made his leg ache. He had hoped that in coming back to Castonbury he would at least have been able to find some peace, to cease to fight the battles of the world. But there could be no peace until this strange matter was dealt with once and for all.

And he was the only one who could do it. It was *his* name that had been used to dishonour his family. He had to end it.

Jamie lowered himself from the high seat and tied the horse up to the garden fence. He watched the house surreptitiously the whole time, pretending to be absorbed in his task, and he was rewarded by the flicker of a curtain at an upstairs window. He glimpsed a flash of pale hair before the fabric fell back in place.

Someone was there, after all. Was she alone?

Jamie pushed open the broken gate and made his way carefully up the overgrown path. The silence seemed to roar around him, the wind through the trees, the rustle of the old, dried leaves and dead flowers under his boots, the creak of the house.

At the door, Jamie rested one hand on his hip where he could feel the weight of his pistol tucked inside his coat and raised the other to knock. The sound echoed hollowly, and for a moment he could hear nothing. Then it came to him, the faintest brush as of slippers on a dusty floor. If his senses hadn't been trained to high alert in Spain, he would have missed it.

Then it went quiet again.

'Miss Walters?' he called gently. 'I know you are there. It's Jamie Montague. I just want to speak with you.'

There was a small rustle again, and then nothing.

'Please, Miss Walters,' he said. 'I mean you

no harm. I don't want to have to return with my brothers, who might not be so peaceable.'

After a long, tense moment, there was the scrape of a lock being drawn back and the door opened a couple of inches. Through the crack Jamie saw a blue muslin skirt and a flash of a pale cheek. She gasped when she saw him, and he thrust his booted foot into the gap in case she decided to slam it shut again.

'It *is* you,' she said hoarsely.

'Yes, it's me,' he answered. 'Not quite as dead as you thought, I fear.'

'How did you find me?'

'I have my ways. Now, please let me in so we can talk in private.' Not that there was anyone to hear but the wind and the trees, but Jamie still didn't want his family's business conducted out of doors.

Alicia glanced back over her shoulder and hesitated. But finally she nodded and pulled the door open all the way.

Jamie stepped into a tiny hall just as she spun around and hurried away. He followed her into a small sitting room, filled with furniture draped in holland covers and an empty fireplace surmounted by a dusty mantel. One settee was uncovered and piled with blankets. Alicia rushed over to it and picked up the child who sat there playing with some wooden blocks, a cherubic toddler with blue eyes and golden curls.

She held him tightly to her shoulder as she turned to face Jamie. Her eyes, the same chinablue as the baby's, were bright with unshed tears but she held her head high.

Jamie remembered her from Spain, how she had scurried so quietly behind Colonel Chambers's noisy wife, how her pale hair and plain clothes had blended into the background. Now she was just as quiet, trembling but calm, and he could scarcely credit she was the same woman who had pulled such a bold, dangerous scheme.

Perhaps Everett was right. Perhaps someone had driven her to it. Perhaps someone had forced her, blackmailed her.

But that didn't change the fact that she *had* done it. And he needed answers.

'Have you come to arrest me?' she asked.

'Not yet,' Jamie answered. As he watched, the child popped his fingers into his little mouth and grinned at Jamie. Jamie could see why his father had loved the child. But it was not his son. Not the son he had once dared to dream of having with Catalina.

'I need to know what happened,' he said.

'We thought you were dead!' Alicia burst out, her calm cracking. 'I didn't think it would hurt anyone, and your father seemed so happy. I only wanted to take care of my little Crispin.'

'Crispin?' Jamie laughed. 'You named him after my father? You *are* bold.'

'I thought you were dead,' Alicia said again.

'So you came up with this whole elaborate scheme all on your own?' Jamie said. 'You found my lost signet ring after it was stolen, forged a marriage licence and found my family. Put the whole plan together and thought you could fool everyone. Very clever.'

'Yes. I—I did it all myself,' she said. But Jamie saw her eyes flicker, her shoulders tense. The baby frowned and fidgeted.

'I don't believe you. Tell me what happened, the truth, and I can help you and your son. But if you don't there is nothing I can do for you and no place where you can hide from me.'

Alicia turned away to put the child back down

on the settee and handed him one of his blocks. Jamie gave her the moment to think, and when she faced him again she nodded.

'There—there was someone who helped me,' she said slowly. 'A friend.'

'He was not much of a friend if he led you into such a crime,' Jamie said. 'And now he appears to have abandoned you here. Unless he is hidden in that cupboard over there.'

'No. He is gone. I don't know where he went, and I…' Alicia broke off on a choked sob. 'He said he knew what to do, how to make all this come out right.'

'Who is it?'

Alicia bit her lip as the tears spilled from her eyes. 'Captain Hugh Webster. You remember him from Spain? He gave me your ring, he told me what to do.'

Webster. Jamie shook his head. He should have known. He remembered playing cards with Webster in Spain. Everyone suspected the man of cheating but no one could prove it. He had always made Jamie feel uneasy in his presence, and now he knew why.

The way the man had stared at Catalina, which

had made Jamie want to call the man out, should have been the only clue he needed to tell him the man was untrustworthy.

'Of course. Webster,' Jamie said. 'And now he has fled to leave you to take his punishment.'

Alicia sat down beside her son, sobbing. 'What will happen to my Crispin now? I know I should not have listened to Webster, I should never have…'

'I will help you, Alicia, if you will help me,' Jamie said. Despite himself he was moved by her tears, by the child clinging to her.

'I would do anything I could to help you, Lord Hatherton, I swear it,' Alicia answered hoarsely. 'But what can I do?'

'You are going to help me find Webster,' Jamie said. He thought of everything his family had been through, he thought of what the strain had done to his father. He could scarcely believe the difference between the strong and formidable man he had said goodbye to and the frail shadow he had come home to. He thought of Giles, taking on a responsibility he had never wanted, having to contend with this false claim under the burden of the failing family finances. He thought of his sisters and what they must have gone through with all the uncertainty. And he thought of his brother Harry, who had come all the way to Seville to find out the truth, of all the hardships he had encountered on his journey. He knew that he bore some responsibility for that, but this man Webster, he must be made to pay. And Jamie knew just how to do it. He would find Webster, and then he would kill him. . . .

Chapter Seven

'Do you think there will be handsome young men at this party, Mrs Moreno?'

Catalina wanted to smile at Lydia Westman's shyly eager words. It was very hard to keep a stern governess demeanour in the face of the girl's enthusiasm, but sternness had to be maintained. Catalina had learned that after weeks of being practically alone with the girl in the countryside before being summoned to this wedding. Lydia was a romantic young lady with a great fondness for horrid novels about ghosts and crumbling castles and lost loves, and she was rather eager to find out what it was like to fall in love herself. Catalina had not been with her very long at all, only a matter of weeks, but she had grown fond of the girl. And she had seen right away that her first task would be to make sure Lydia employed a bit of sense in who she chose to marry.

Unlike Catalina herself, who had thought nothing of throwing herself headlong into wild wartime romance—and paid the price with her heart, which was now locked safely away.

'I am sure there will be,' Catalina said, bracing herself as the carriage jounced over another rut in the road. Lydia didn't seem to notice, as she had been buried in her latest volume of romantic poetry for several miles, leaving Catalina to her own thoughts. 'It is a wedding, after all. I'm sure the bridegroom has many young relatives and friends.'

'And a wedding in a great family!' Lydia said with a sigh. 'I can't believe I have never met them before, even though the duchess was my mother's cousin. My friend Miss Crompton told me the Montagues are said to be most peculiar. Do you suppose that means there is *madness* in the family? I have never met a real mad person before. It should be most interesting, don't you think, Mrs Moreno?'

Catalina bit her lip to keep from laughing. 'I am sure they are no more peculiar than any other ducal family. Such people are entitled to their eccentricities, I believe, especially here in England.'

'Do you not have dukes in Spain, Mrs Moreno?'

'Of course we do. But they are rather different.' Catalina drew a volume of *Don Quixote* from her valise and handed it to Lydia. 'Why do you not read that for a while? There are lots of mad people in that tale, and you can practise your Spanish a bit. You have been doing so well with it.' Learning languages was one of the reasons Lydia's guardian had hired a foreign companion for her, that and Mrs Burnes's stellar recommendation.

Lydia frowned as she turned the book over in her hands. 'It looks rather...long.'

'We still have some time before we reach Castonbury.'

Lydia nodded and opened the volume, and as Catalina had expected she was soon lost in the don's adventures with Sancho Panza. And Catalina was left alone again.

She gazed out of the carriage window as the scenery bounced past. It was so green and soft, so very different from the rolling brown hills and enclosed gardens of Spain.

But *different* was what she had sought when she had fled Spain. There was nothing for her there. Even if she had sought to reclaim her family's place, her well-known anti-monarchical ideas would have made life in Spain uncomfortable. And she had little money. When the chance had come to travel to England as nurse to an English general's sickly wife, it had seemed like an opportunity. A chance to begin life again after all that had happened.

Even though it meant beginning in England, Jamie's homeland. Yet she had never imagined her new position, as governess and companion to a pretty debutante, would take her to his actual home. She had only got the job thanks to Mrs Burnes's glowing reference and had known little about the task at first. She and Lydia had been staying in the countryside, away from Town gossip.

Castonbury. She remembered how he had spoken of it, his family's home, and it hadn't sounded like it could be a real place. It had sounded like a whole world in itself, a green land of lakes and follies and hidden bowers. Catalina had loved his tales of it, because her own home was gone and she had never really felt like she belonged there anyway. She didn't belong anywhere, except for those few moments in Jamie's arms when she hadn't been able to imagine being anywhere else.

But that had been an illusion in the end, a dream she had conjured up all on her own. The only reality in life was to be alone. Twice widowed, she had learned that well, and she was content with it. She had learned to put Jamie away, hidden deep in her heart. To forget about what had been—and what might have been, if he had come back and they had been able to work things out between them. If everything had been as she dreamed.

Never had she thought she would go to his home and see his family. When Lydia's guardian had asked her to go with the girl for this wedding, her first instinct had been to refuse, to quit her position and find a new one where she would never have to see this place. Never be so starkly reminded of Jamie, and how her dreams had been shattered by his work and then by his death.

Catalina looked across the carriage at Lydia. The girl had her head bent over her book, the daylight playing over the red-gold curls that peeked from under her chip straw bonnet. Catalina *liked* Lydia. In truth, she had become quite fond of her in the short time they had been together, and she sensed that Lydia needed her. The girl had been motherless for a long time, and in her one Season weathering the storm of Society life hadn't been easy for her. Catalina couldn't just leave her.

Even if it did mean going to Castonbury.

It is only for a few days, Catalina told herself. Just a few days in a house that she would surely find was only a house, a place of stone and brick where no trace of Jamie remained. She would be quiet and unobtrusive, as she always was, and the family would take no notice of her.

Then they would go back to London and it would be over.

As if she sensed Catalina watching her, Lydia glanced up and smiled. But it wasn't her usual sunny smile. It seemed strangely tentative.

'Is something wrong, *pequeña*?' Catalina asked.

Lydia shook her head. 'No, of course not. What could be wrong? I just…'

'Just what?'

'I just wonder—will they like me? The Montagues?' Lydia sounded so young and unsure.

'Of course they will like you,' Catalina said. 'They are your family.'

'I know, but they don't really *feel* like my family. I hardly know them at all. I mean, I met the duchess once when I was a child, though I scarcely remember her, and Lady Kate came to call when she had her Season, but that's all. I'm not sure why they even invited me to this wedding.'

'Perhaps because they want to know you better?' Catalina said soothingly. 'I am sure there is nothing to fear. You need only enjoy yourself for a few days and get to know your relatives. You are sure to like them, and they can't help but like you.'

Lydia bit her lip. 'Do you think so?'

'I am sure of it.' Catalina gave her a smile. 'And I am sure there will be handsome young men there, just as you hoped.'

Lydia laughed. 'Oh, I do hope so! If I can only be brave enough to talk to them.'

'You need have no fear of that. *They* will talk to *you*.' Catalina tapped the book in Lydia's hands.

'Now, tell me what you think of the don. Have you any Spanish words you want to go over?'

They talked about the story until the carriage slowed down to sway around a bend in the road. Catalina looked out the window and saw they were rolling through a pair of elaborately wrought iron gates surmounted by a family crest.

Castonbury. They were here at last.

The ornate iron gates, surmounted by the family crest and with a substantial stone lodge nearby, stood open to greet guests. Vast gardens lay beyond in a rolling vista of beautiful views, with twin lakes in the distance connected by an arched bridge and with white marble follies on hilltops. It was all just as Jamie had said it was.

Catalina swallowed hard as they drew closer to the house. It looked as if it had been just there on the land for ever, a graceful, classical sweep of a house, pale and perfect and somehow as substantial as a mountain. It proclaimed that it belonged there, that its family belonged there. It spoke of tradition and duty and devotion.

And Catalina could see so clearly now that she could *never* have belonged there as the Montagues did. Even if Jamie had lived and brought her here as his marchioness, it would not have been hers.

'Mrs Moreno?' Lydia asked, her voice soft with concern. 'Are you quite well? You look so strange all of a sudden.'

Catalina turned away from the window and smiled at Lydia. 'I am perfectly fine. I think I've just been in the carriage too long and need some fresh air. Isn't the house lovely?'

'Oh, yes!' Lydia turned eagerly to the view, her eyes shining as she took in the prospect down the sweep of the drive. 'I have heard about Castonbury for ages, and it is just as I imagined it. It looks as if a king should live there.'

A king. A memory suddenly flashed through Catalina's mind, of Jamie walking with her beside a Spanish river, the sunlight gleaming on his dark hair and turning his skin to pure, molten gold. In that moment when everything seemed to go still around them, she had been sure he looked like a god come to earth.

The carriage drew to a halt, and Catalina was pulled out of her memories and into the present moment. She wasn't here to remember, she was here to work, to get through these few days and get on with her life again. She straightened the ribbons of her bonnet and smoothed down the collar of her grey pelisse.

A footman hurried to open the carriage door and lower the steps. Catalina stepped down onto the gravel drive behind Lydia, and had to grab the girl's arm before she could go dashing off to look at some horses in a nearby paddock. Lydia had never had the chance to learn to really ride and yet was fascinated by horses.

'We must greet our hostess and find our rooms first, Lydia, don't forget,' Catalina said. 'There will be time for exploring later.'

Lydia pouted a bit, but she obediently followed Catalina up the wide stone steps and through the pillared portico into the front doors. The soaring hall was so dark and gloomy that for a moment Catalina couldn't see anything at all. She felt like she was surrounded by shadows, by the sweet smell of flowers and beeswax polish pressing in on her.

She rubbed her gloved hand over her eyes and looked up to see a staircase winding into the upper recesses of the house. Marble pillars lined the space, soaring up to a painted ceiling and more galleries above. Paintings in heavy gilt frames were hung on the panelled wall along its length, an array of Elizabethan ruffs and Cavalier plumes mixed with powdered wigs and satin gowns. And one young man standing under a tree in the Castonbury Park, his hat held casually in his hand as the breeze tousled his dark hair and he smiled out at the viewer.

Jamie. It was Jamie, younger and more carefree than when she had known him, but just as handsome. Just as wondrously alive, before Spain had altered his soul.

Her throat tightened, and she turned away from the glow of those blue-grey eyes. Perhaps being here at Castonbury would be harder than she had feared.

'Miss Westman?' a woman asked. Catalina turned to see a lady hurrying towards them. 'I am Mrs Stratton, housekeeper at Castonbury. Welcome to the estate.'

'Thank you,' Lydia said, and Catalina was proud of her calm poise. 'It is most lovely here.'

'Miss Seagrove was very sorry not to be here to greet you herself, but she and the other ladies went into Buxton for the day. I will have some tea sent to your room, and everyone should be here for dinner this evening. If you would care to follow me.' Mrs Stratton turned to smile at Catalina. 'And you are Mrs Moreno, yes?'

'Yes, I am,' Catalina answered. 'I am also very pleased to be here.'

'I have put your room right across from Miss Westman,' Mrs Stratton said. 'I hope that will be comfortable for you both?'

Catalina had half expected to be sent off to the servants' quarters where it would be next to impossible to keep an eye on Lydia. She was quite pleasantly surprised. 'Yes, of course. Most comfortable.'

'You both must be tired from your journey. I will show you to your rooms directly.' Mrs Stratton led them up the staircase, the keys at her belt jangling lightly. 'The rest of the guests will arrive tomorrow.'

Catalina looked away from Jamie as they passed his portrait, but it was almost as if he watched her walk past. As if he was with her here in his house.

She took a deep breath and tried to focus on Lydia and not the strangeness of being in Jamie's home. For once the girl was perfectly silent, staring around her with wide eyes as they turned down a corridor lined with more paintings, more carved furniture, more Chinese vases filled with bright flowers and classical statues set in their niches. They passed several closed doors and a maid hurrying past with a tray in her hands until they came to the end of the corridor.

'I hope you will like it here,' Mrs Stratton said as she opened one of the doors. 'It is quietest at this end of the guest wing.'

Lydia's room was lovely, a charming space with a white-draped bed and modern French furniture grouped around a tiled fireplace. A maid was already laying out her things on the tulle-covered dressing table. The windows looked out on the terraced gardens behind the house, rolling down to the twin lakes joined by a bridge.

'It's beautiful.' Lydia sighed. She leaned against the windowsill to peer outside, still wide-eyed at the beauty of the place.

'Let me show you to your room, Mrs Moreno,' Mrs Stratton said. 'Sally can help Miss Westman while you settle in.'

'Thank you,' Catalina said. She followed the

housekeeper to the room across the corridor, suddenly weary. The journey had been a long one, and now being in this house weighed on her heavily. She rubbed her eyes and stepped into the chamber across the corridor.

It was smaller than Lydia's and looked out onto a smaller side garden, but it was just as comfortably furnished with a dark wood bed and tables and chairs upholstered with blue velvet. A cushioned seat was built into the window, a perfect spot for curling up to read or nap.

Catalina laughed—there would be no time for napping if she was to keep up with Lydia.

'I do hope this will be convenient for you, Mrs Moreno. I do know how…complicated it can be to watch over young ladies,' Mrs Stratton said. She stopped to straighten some of the *objets* on the mantel. 'There were no adjoining rooms available with all the people here for the wedding, but hopefully Miss Westman is near enough.'

'This is perfect, thank you,' Catalina said. She watched as Mrs Stratton slid a framed image from behind a pair of porcelain shepherdesses and brushed it off. Catalina was startled to see that it was a copy of the same pastel portrait that Jamie carried with him in Spain. His two sisters smiling out of the image with their grey Montague eyes.

Mrs Stratton seemed to notice Catalina staring at it, for she said, 'They are very pretty girls, are they not?'

Catalina swallowed before she could answer. 'Very pretty.'

'Lady Kate and Lady Phaedra. Lady Kate is in Boston now with her new husband, but you will meet Lady Phaedra and her husband, Bram. She is usually outdoors with her horses, but she does manage to make it to family dinners, especially now.' Mrs Stratton laughed.

'I am sure Miss Westman will greatly enjoy meeting her,' Catalina answered. 'She does love animals, but there is seldom a chance for her to spend time with them in London.'

'You yourself are Spanish, are you not, Mrs Moreno?'

'Yes, I am. My family was from Seville.'

'Have you been in London long?'

'A while now. But sometimes it feels a lot longer,' Catalina said with a smile. 'I have been in the country these past few weeks with Lydia, very isolated.'

'If you feel homesick, there will be plenty of people here to talk about Spain with, Mrs Moreno. I dare say they would appreciate the chance to talk about their travels as well.' The small clock on the mantel chimed and Mrs Stratton gave it a startled glance. 'Oh, dear! Is that the time? You must excuse me. There is so much to see to before dinner. I will have a tea tray sent to you right away.'

Once the housekeeper was gone, Catalina wearily untied her bonnet and laid it aside with her gloves. She sat down on the window seat and peered out at the garden below. It was green and pretty, rolling down to a line of trees and dotted with marble benches and statues. Gardeners were scurrying between the flower beds, as if to make it all even more beautiful for the wedding.

It was all so much as she had imagined it when Jamie would tell her about this house. Green and classical, the perfect place for rambling walks and picnics. Casual and elegant at the same time, so different from the highly regimented gardens she was used to in Spain.

As she watched, a figure suddenly appeared atop a low rise beyond the dip of the ha-ha. It was too far for her to see his features, and he had a wide-brimmed hat pulled low over his brow. But he was tall and lean, his athletic figure clad in a long, dark jacket. He held a walking stick in one hand. For an instant, with the sunlight behind him, Catalina thought it was Jamie and she couldn't breathe.

He paused to peer out over the gardens, perfectly still, and Catalina dared not move. She knew it was an illusion, that the man must merely be one of Jamie's brothers or another guest, but ever since she had come through the Castonbury gates she had felt strangely near to him. She wanted to hold on to that for just a moment longer, and imagine what he was like here.

Then the man walked down the hill, his gait slightly uneven though he barely used the stick. He vanished around the side of the house and out of her sight, and the brief dream was shattered. Jamie, the good and the bad of their time together, was gone.

Catalina closed her eyes and leaned her forehead against the cool glass of the window. She wished this wedding would be over very quickly indeed. It was obvious she needed to escape from Castonbury before she went mad.

Chapter Eight

'Are you sure my gown is quite right, Mrs Moreno?' Lydia whispered as they made their way down the staircase.

Catalina gave her a reassuring smile. 'You look lovely,' she said truthfully. Lydia looked like a blooming summer rose in her pale pink muslin, with pink and white ribbons twined in her shining curls. Catalina could scarcely remember ever being so young and fresh, so eager to see what life held next. She had felt like an old lady for so long. Too long.

She caught a glimpse of herself as they passed an antique looking glass on the wall, and for an instant she thought she was a ghost in her grey taffeta gown, her hair twisted back in a plain knot. Once Lydia was safely married, Catalina knew she should try do something fun in her life again, something interesting. Not just another position, but something *real*, like when she had been nursing in Spain.

Catalina almost laughed aloud at herself. What else was there she could do but keep working? Keep taking each day as it came? That was her life now, and she was content with it. At least it didn't hurt as it had when she lost Jamie. When she lost her husband.

'I do want them to like me,' Lydia said as she smoothed her white satin sash again.

'They cannot help but like you,' Catalina answered. 'They are your family, are they not?'

Lydia glanced at her with wide eyes. 'I suppose they are, though I hardly know them. I think I never really had a family. Just my guardian, and he's only my father's grumpy old great-uncle, you know.'

'Well, now you do have a family. And it's a large one, if all the portraits we've seen today are any indication.'

Lydia was silent for a moment. 'Do you miss your family greatly, Mrs Moreno?'

Catalina looked away. Aside from talking in a

general way about Spanish history and literature, she had never spoken of her old life to Lydia. It seemed better to keep that all in the past, hidden away. It must be this house, with all its history and memories that made them both feel so wistful.

'I do miss them sometimes,' she said. 'But my parents and my poor brother have been gone now for many years. And they would have been terribly unhappy about what has happened to our country if they could see it.'

'What of your husband? Do you miss him?'

For one startled instant, Catalina thought she meant Jamie. Her throat tightened and she could only stare at Lydia in silence.

'Do you not miss Mr Moreno?' Lydia asked.

Of course. Her first husband. As far as anyone knew, her only husband, and it would have to stay that way. The opulent history of Castonbury, the weight of family and tradition, seemed to press in around her, and she realised again how foolish she and Jamie had been to ever think they could make a future together. She could not have belonged here. They would have made each other unhappy and their passion would have faded. She would have remembered his work in Spain, and he would remember how she opposed him.

'He has also been gone a long time,' she said quietly. 'He was much older than me, and we were not married long. Our families had wanted an alliance for many years.' And when her brother died opposing the king, that alliance had seemed even more important.

'How dreadful,' Lydia declared. 'I shall not marry like that. I shall only marry someone I love.'

Catalina smiled at her. 'I do hope so, my dear. Only you must fall in love with someone who can also take proper care of you.'

They reached the main hall, and a balding man with protuberant eyes and a black coat stepped out of the shadows to bow to them.

'Miss Westman, Mrs Moreno—I am Lumsden, butler here at Castonbury,' he said in a stentorious, deeply important voice. 'The others are gathered in the drawing room, if I may show you the way.'

'Thank you, Lumsden,' Catalina answered. Lydia seemed struck silent again.

Lumsden bowed again and led them down

another series of grand corridors. Castonbury seemed full of such spaces, lined with fine *objets d'art* and paintings, with jewel-like carpets on the floors and a few old tapestries on the walls. But Catalina couldn't help noticing that here and there were empty spaces, as if whatever had sat there for years and years had been taken away. Some of the draperies and upholsteries were worn, and a few patches of plaster on the moulded ceilings needed to be repaired.

She glanced at another faded square on the wallpaper where a painting had once hung. It could just have been taken down for repair or restoration, of course, but—was Castonbury in some kind of trouble after losing its heir?

Catalina looked at the girl beside her. Lydia had a fine but not exorbitant dowry. But perhaps any amount of money would be useful enough here for her to make a match with one of the Montagues? If there were any unmatched males left, that was. Perhaps the girl's dreams of true love would have to be replaced by ducal strawberry leaves if that was the case.

She could hear the buzz of voices and laughter before Lumsden even opened the drawing room door. They stepped into a vast chamber with soaring ceilings decorated with elaborate white plasterwork and walls papered in blue silk and hung with landscapes and portraits. A fire burned in the white marble grate, and gilded blue damask sofas and chairs were scattered in groupings around the room, interspersed with tables laden with figurines and enamelled boxes and vases. A pianoforte and a harp sat in the corner.

But the elegance of the room was overshadowed by the people who gathered around the space. They were all laughing and talking exuberantly, the gloomy silence of the house banished.

Lydia gave Catalina a look that seemed distinctly frightened. Catalina smiled and gave her arm a little squeeze, but she had to admit she herself felt a little nervous faced with so many Montagues.

A lady broke away from the crowd and came towards them, her green silk gown shimmering.

'You must be Miss Westman,' the lady said with a kind smile. 'I have been looking forward to meeting you. I am Lily Seagrove.'

The bride. Catalina studied her with interest, this lady who was marrying into the family she herself had once so briefly dreamed of joining. She seemed kind and welcoming, her eyes warm as she smiled.

'How do you do,' Lydia said, and gave her a small curtsey with a poise that made Catalina proud. 'I am happy to meet you as well. This is my companion, Mrs Moreno.'

'Of course,' Lily said, turning her friendly smile to Catalina. 'We have heard so much about you. My brother-in-law Lord Harry and his wife, Elena, have talked of nothing but how they look forward to meeting you. They have recently returned from Spain themselves for the wedding, though soon they will be off to their new posting. He is in the diplomatic service.'

'I look forward to meeting them then,' Catalina said politely, though in truth she wasn't sure if talking about Spain would make her more or less homesick, more or less full of memories. She didn't want to remember old hopes for her country and how they had been shattered in reality.

'Then you must meet them now!' Lily declared. 'Come, let me introduce you both to everyone.'

Lily led them around the room and made the introductions to the people gathered there. There were so many of them that Catalina was quite sure she would never remember them all. There was the bridegroom, Lord Giles, a tall, handsome man with the same grey eyes most of the Montagues seemed to possess. His smile was so tender, so full of happiness, when he looked at his bride that it made Catalina's heart ache to see it. They just seemed to *belong* together, to fit in a way so few couples did.

There was Lady Phaedra, Jamie's sister, who Catalina remembered from the portrait Jamie carried, and her husband, Bram Basingstoke, who held her hand while she talked. Phaedra asked Catalina if she rode, and, on hearing that she had used to enjoy it very much but hadn't had the chance in years, told her that she must come and inspect the facilities that were being built for Phaedra's new stud at Castonbury.

'I would enjoy that very much,' Catalina said, and indeed she would. She missed riding, and Lady Phaedra's great enthusiasm was infectious. She added quietly enough that Lydia could not hear, 'But I fear Miss Westman has not had many chances to ride and isn't sure how, though she is very curious about horses. She has lived all her life in London.'

'Hasn't been able to ride much?' Phaedra gasped, her eyes large with shock. 'Good heavens. Well, she is in the country now. We must teach her. You should both come to the stables with me first thing after the wedding.'

Her husband laughed and squeezed her hand. 'My dear, they will probably be quite busy with everything that is going on at Castonbury. Touring the stables many not be first on their list.'

Phaedra gave a rueful laugh. 'Of course, Mrs Moreno, Miss Westman. I do get rather carried away when I talk about my horses. But you must come and ride with me any time you choose. I have the sweetest, kindest little mare that should just suit Miss Westman.'

'That is very kind of you,' Catalina answered. Lydia still looked too terrified to say much at all.

They were led around the room again to meet yet more people, including a plethora of guests who had come in from the village and neighbouring houses for the dinner. There was also Lord Harry, the diplomatic son, and his wife, Elena, who declared herself so full of happiness to meet a countrywoman and said they had to sit down for a long talk as soon as possible. Not as congenial was Mrs Landes-Fraser ('Aunt Wilhemina,' Lily whispered with a shiver), an elderly lady ensconced by the fire and swathed in layers of silk, Indian shawls and a plumed turban, despite the warm evening.

She inspected them closely before snorting. 'Pretty enough,' she declared of Lydia, 'but much too pale. Like your mother, are you, girl? She had no spirit either.'

Lily led them away from 'Aunt Wilhemina' as quickly as she could with an apologetic smile. 'You must not mind her,' she whispered. 'She is that way with absolutely everyone. I was terrified of her when I first came to Castonbury.'

Catalina saw that Lydia regained her 'spirit' quickly enough when they met a certain Mr Hale, a handsome young man with a cap of bright blond hair and friendly eyes who was the new curate at the Castonbury church. He eagerly bowed over Lydia's hand and smiled down at her as she stared up at him.

Catalina could see at one glance that this was a situation that called for a close watch.

'Mr Hale has only been here a short time,' Lily said. 'But the vicar, my adoptive father Reverend Seagrove, cannot stop singing his praises. He has certainly brought a new life to the parish.'

'You are too kind, Miss Seagrove,' Mr Hale said with a smile. He still smiled at Lydia. 'I am only doing my duty.'

'I am sure you are absolutely marvellous at it, Mr Hale,' Lydia said softly.

'Where is the duke?' Mrs Landes-Fraser suddenly cried. 'It is past time for supper to be served. I don't know why he suddenly insists on eating with us anyway. Most inconvenient after all this time. I shall need to eat soon or my digestion won't be able to bear it.'

'I'm sure Father will be here very soon,' Phaedra said. 'You know how excited he is about all that has happened. It's like he has a new life in him.'

Mrs Landes-Fraser gave another snort and adjusted her shawls around her. 'New life? Hmph! We were doing just fine with the way our life was before.'

Phaedra frowned and looked as if she very

much wanted to argue, but the drawing room door opened before she could say anything.

Catalina glanced towards the man who had just come into the room. It had to be the duke himself, an imposing man with faded dark hair and clothes that looked a bit too large for him.

'About time,' Mrs Landes-Fraser muttered.

Harry stepped to his father's side. 'Here, Father, let me help you to your chair by the fire.'

The duke shook him away. 'I am quite all right, my boy. Quit fussing so.' His sharp grey eyes, half hidden under lowered brows, suddenly focused on Lydia. 'And who is this, then? Must be Miss Westman, eh?'

Lydia gave a little squeak, and Catalina squeezed her hand to hold her still.

'I—I am Miss Westman, Your Grace,' Lydia said, and managed a wobbling curtsey.

'Well, come here, girl—let me get a closer look at you,' the duke barked.

Lydia had just taken one slow step in his direction when another man moved into the room behind him. He moved so quietly, keeping to the shadow of the door so that no one seemed to notice him. But something seemed to close around

Catalina's heart as soon as she glimpsed him and she slid closer involuntarily.

Surely—no, no, it could not. It had to be another Montague brother, or perhaps a cousin, and just being in this house had made her overly imaginative. It had already happened more than once. She had been thinking about him too much and now she thought she did see him. That was all it was.

But—but there was something about the man who stood there at the edge of the room so very still. Something watchful that reminded her of Jamie. And he looked so very much like him with that close-cropped dark hair, those strong shoulders under the finely cut coat.

'James, come and meet Miss Westman,' the duke called with an imperious wave of his hand.

James. As Catalina watched dizzily, the man stepped forward. He didn't have Jamie's graceful, panther-like movements; he limped a bit, but still that impression remained. Catalina felt icy cold, frozen to the spot as she watched him come nearer. She shrank back into the shadows as much as she could.

But he saw her. His eyes widened and then

narrowed, and a muscle tensed along his jaw. He bowed to Lydia, yet his stare never wavered from Catalina.

'Miss Westman,' he said. 'I'm always pleased to meet a new-found relative.'

'Miss Westman, this is Lord Hatherton, my almost brother-in-law,' Lily said quickly. 'And, Jamie, this is Miss Westman's companion, Mrs Moreno.'

Jamie straightened to his full tall height and looked directly into Catalina's eyes, and she saw that it really *was* him. Her husband, who she had so long thought dead. She pressed her hand to her throat and shook her head.

'Madre de Dios,' she whispered. Jamie? Here, alive. No, it could not be. She was asleep and dreaming. The journey had tired her and she was imagining things again, just like with that man in the garden.

But then he took her cold, limp hand in his and looked at her with those bright grey eyes. She felt his skin against hers, so warm, so real. So alive. Not a dream, not a vision that would dissolve when she awoke.

'Catalina,' he whispered so only she could hear. His voice, too, was real, just as she remembered it.

The whole crowded room spun around her, and there was such a roaring in her ears, like a dozen rushing rivers. Just like the river that had supposedly swallowed him up. She stumbled back against the nearest table, her legs too weak to hold her up.

'You're not going to swoon, are you, Catalina? Not now,' Jamie said. His voice was exactly the same, just as she heard it so often in her haunted dreams. Rough and warm all at the same time.

'No,' she managed to say, just before darkness closed in around her and she felt herself falling and falling.

Until strong arms closed around her.

She came to when she heard Lydia sobbing and crying, 'Mrs Moreno! Oh, Mrs Moreno, please wake up.'

'Give the lady some air, for heaven's sake,' Lady Phaedra said impatiently.

'I have my vinaigrette,' Aunt Wilhemina said. 'No one should ever go anywhere without their vinaigrette. Here, James, give her this.'

Catalina tried to open her eyes, to tell them all

she was quite all right, but she felt so very cold. She couldn't quit shivering. And she felt so silly. She never fainted, not even during her nursing duties in Spain when there had been blood and limbs everywhere.

'I think she is in shock,' Jamie said. He sounded so calm, just as he had whenever a crisis threatened in the military camps, but there was tremor running just beneath the words. 'Everyone move aside, please. Phaedra is right, she does need some air. It is much too warm in here.'

Jamie scooped her up in his arms and Catalina felt him carry her across the drawing room and nudge open a door with his shoulder. The noise of everyone arguing over the best way to treat a faint faded behind them.

He lowered her carefully until she felt satin cushions at her back and she finally opened her eyes. He had carried her into a small sitting room crowded with furniture, and the only light was the silvery glow of the moon from beyond the window. He leaned over her, watching her in silence, and she stared up at him in the moonlight. He was a stranger, yet once he had been her husband.

He was certainly as handsome as ever, tall and

elegantly lean, dark and bright all at the same time. Yet there was something there that had not been in the man she married. Deep lines bracketed his sensual mouth. His grey eyes were so wary, as flat and still as a millpond, hiding his emotions. It was almost as if another soul had come to inhabit the body of the man she loved.

Was her Jamie still behind those dead eyes? What had happened to him? Had he finished his work in Spain? Above all—how was he here, alive, when he had been gone for so long?

'I—I thought you dead,' she managed to say. 'They told me you were drowned that day.'

'Catalina. What an impasse,' he said quietly. 'I thought *you* were dead.'

She stared up at him, aghast at his words. 'You thought I was dead? Why?'

'After the river, and many days in a makeshift field hospital nearby, I managed to make my way back to the camp, but it had been destroyed. I found a farmer who told me the French had attacked the contingent who had been left behind after we departed, that almost everyone had been killed—including the surgeon you worked with and the chaplain who married us. He showed me the place where they buried everyone. He showed be *your* grave. And he gave me…this.'

Jamie untied his cravat and reached inside his shirt to draw out a thin gold chain. The moonlight caught on the object that dangled from it, a sapphire ring. 'He was an honest man indeed to give it up,' he said quietly. 'I knew you would not have parted from it willingly.'

Catalina rubbed at her bare finger and closed her eyes as the terror of that long-ago day washed over her again. She remembered so well running, fleeing blindly to she knew not where until she found that hidey-hole in the woods. By then it was too late to go back and search for her precious ring. All that she had left of Jamie.

But Jamie was *here*. And he wore her ring. Surely that meant something. Anything.

She opened her eyes again, only to find that he still looked down at her with that steady stillness, that lack of expression that made him resemble one of the marble statues that dotted Castonbury's lush gardens. Jamie was so different here, like an entirely separate person from the man she had married. What had happened to him? Where was he?

What was he capable of, this man she had once thought she knew so well and then turned out not to know at all?

Perhaps the ring was not a memento of her, then. Perhaps it was merely to remind him not to make the mistake of marrying in haste again.

Slowly, cautiously, she reached up and brushed the scar on his face with her fingertips. It felt rough under her touch, but his skin was so warm. So real. He tensed, that muscle in his jaw flexing, but he didn't pull away.

'Where did you go after that?' she whispered. 'What have you been doing?' Had he done his task of restoring the king to the Spanish throne? What lengths had he gone to in order to do that?

'That is not important,' he answered, his voice low and rough. 'I can hardly think of anything tonight. It has all been turned upside down.'

Catalina nodded. She knew how that felt—it seemed like a hundred years since she had walked downstairs with Lydia. The moment before and the moment after she saw him again marked a vast chasm of time. Right now she felt as if she floated free in the night sky, untethered to any kind of reality at all.

Jamie took her hand in his with a terrible gentleness and held her fingers on his palm as he studied them. 'Why did you come to England? Did you journey here alone, or on some mission?'

Catalina stared at him. Just like him, she couldn't remember why she had come to England, or anything else. Just him, just this moment. 'I came to England because I couldn't bear Spain any longer. With the Bourbons returned—it was not my home, you know. I wanted to make a new start here.'

'Ah, yes. I remember how you hated the king.' Jamie carefully laid her hand back at her side. 'You were so passionate about it.'

And she suddenly recalled how *he* had been meant to help restore the monarchy, to send Spain back to the terrible torpor it had known before Napoleon, with no chance for a new start. Until he died.

'Jamie, what did you…' she began, only to break off when a soft knock sounded at the door. It was as if the cold knife of reality sliced into the moment with Jamie and shattered it.

'Jamie?' Lily called. 'Is Mrs Moreno quite all right?'

'Come in,' Jamie answered. He rose from the settee and moved over to the empty fireplace. He turned his back to Catalina and braced his fore-arm on the mantel.

Catalina pushed herself up until she could swing her feet down to the floor just as Lily slipped into the room. She held a goblet in her hand.

'Goodness, but it is dark in here,' she said, but she seemed calm and not shocked at all that a man and a woman would be in a dim room together. 'Are you feeling better, Mrs Moreno? Everyone is quite worried, especially Miss Westman.'

Lydia. How could she have forgot? Catalina quickly stood up, only to sway dizzily as her head swam. 'I must go to her.'

'Not until you feel better,' Lily said. 'She is very well looked after by Phaedra and Elena. Here, drink some of this.'

'I feel so foolish,' Catalina murmured as she sipped at the cool water. It helped steady her, but she was still all too aware of Jamie standing there by the fireplace. So near yet so very far away.

'Nonsense. It's always far too stuffy in the drawing room, and you have had a long day.'

Lily slanted a glance at Jamie. 'You moved very quickly to catch her, Jamie.'

He gave them a wry smile over his shoulder. 'I am not so useless, then. I can still rescue damsels in distress.'

'You will surely be kept busy around here, then,' Lily said.

Catalina set her empty glass down on the nearest table. 'I feel quite well now. I should rejoin Miss Westman.'

'I will walk with you,' Lily said. 'Jamie, will you join us?'

'In a moment,' he said, his back turned again.

Catalina gave a lingering glance at his silent figure. There were still so very many things to say, things that could fill days and days. She still longed to wrap her arms around him and hold him close, and know that he was real and not just another dream. That he was real, both the good and the bad.

But this was not the moment. They couldn't be alone, not without everyone in the house knowing it, and she didn't want gossip or speculation. She followed Lily from the small sitting room and back down the corridor to where Lydia and the others waited.

Yet her head still spun with only one confusing, fantastical, glorious thought. *Jamie was alive.*

Catalina was alive.

Jamie braced his fists on the fireplace mantel and fought against the surge of fierce emotion that swept through him. He wasn't even sure what he felt, it was all so tangled up. Joy, shock, appalled fascination. But in the end it just came down to those three powerful words.

Catalina was alive. His wife was alive.

Jamie stared down blindly into the empty grate. He saw her again as she was when he first glimpsed her across that crowded army camp, laughing in the brilliant Spanish sunshine. The most beautiful thing he had ever seen. He remembered how he had wanted that laughter, craved it as he never had anything else. Those days with her had been magic, the most perfect he had ever known.

In the end it was all destroyed, vanished in the face of the reality of what they were living through in the midst of war and upheaval. Then she was dead, gone. And he had gone on to do things she would have hated him for.

He thought again of the pain in her dark eyes when he had told her of his work to bring the Bourbons back to Spain. Then the vision melted into Catalina as he had seen her tonight.

For an instant he had almost thought she was a ghost, come to Castonbury to haunt him as he struggled to make a new life here with the family he no longer belonged to. She was so quiet, hovering at the edges of the crowd in her grey gown, that he imagined he was the only one who could see her. But she had smiled at the young lady who stood beside her, and he had seen a flash of his Catalina again. She was real, she was there, miraculously deposited into his own home.

He almost shouted out her name as a wondrous exultation flashed in his heart. It was as if his life, so cold and pale for so long, turned back to vivid colour and he felt the heat of it on his skin, in his blood. In his very soul. The only place he had ever belonged was *there*. He wanted to run to her, hold her in his arms and feel her body warm and real against his.

Until she looked at him—and turned as white

as if she was a real ghost. He saw only shock in her eyes, and then she had fainted at his feet.

When everyone cried out and gathered around her, all his family, he remembered where they were. In the drawing room at Castonbury. No one knew about her, about Catalina and their impetuous marriage. And the family had only just been rid of one of his supposed wives. And imposter, for sure. But now it was Giles and Lily's moment, a moment they had waited for for a long time. Because of him, his absence, his supposed death, his supposed wife, the near-collapse of the family fortune... He was responsible for delaying their happiness. And his father was still fragile, despite all his bluster. Jamie couldn't just shout out, 'There is my wife!'

No matter how much he wanted to.

But even more than his family, what held him back was Catalina herself. The frightened look in her eyes, the way she had trembled when he touched her. No matter how vivid his memories were, they had been apart for a long time. So much had happened since he last saw her. He had done so much he was not proud of. What had *she* been doing all this time? And how had she escaped the camp when so many had not? When she had known things others had not, because he had confided in her.

Jamie pounded his fist on the mantel. There was so very much they needed to talk about. Years' worth. She was his wife, whether she wanted to be or not.

What was he going to do about that? What did she want from him now?

There was a brisk knock at the door, and he turned around just as Phaedra poked her head inside.

'We're all going in to dinner now, except for Mrs Moreno,' she said. 'Lily insisted she go straight to bed with some ridiculous posset Lily's old Gypsy grandmother, Mrs Lovell, used to make.'

'Mrs Moreno has retired?' he said. He thought he sounded calm and indifferent but perhaps not, as Phaedra frowned as she looked at him. His sister often seemed as if she was completely distracted by her horses, but Jamie knew she was always most aware of everything around her.

'Yes,' she said. 'Does that make you more or less inclined to come to dinner?'

'Of course I am coming to dinner,' Jamie said irritably. Dinner with his family and a gaggle of guests, all gaping at him like he was a creature in a menagerie, sounded unbearable.

And so did knowing Catalina was somewhere in the house and he could not be with her.

'Then you may want to retie your cravat,' Phaedra said matter-of-factly.

Jamie glanced down to see that his cravat was indeed still untied and the ring hung against his shirt. He laughed ruefully and got himself put together again. Once he looked somewhat respectable, he offered Phaedra his arm and they started towards the dining room.

'It feels almost as if Castonbury has become a small Spain of sorts,' she said. 'What with you and Harry just now home from there, and Elena, and now Miss Westman's mysterious companion. Most interesting.'

'Can you even find Spain on a globe, Phaedra?' Jamie teased.

She laughed. 'Of course I can. They have the most astonishing Andalusian horses there. I would love to import some for Castonbury. Perhaps Mrs

Moreno knows something about them. I must talk to her more.'

Jamie had the suspicious feeling that horses were not the only thing Phaedra wanted to talk about with Catalina. He needed to see his wife again and get some answers—soon.

Chapter Nine

'I cannot tell you how happy I am you have come to Castonbury,' Elena Montague said to Catalina in Spanish. They strolled together around the banks of the ornamental lake after an afternoon picnic. The others were still lying about in the shade, finishing the lemonade and the cook's fine almond cakes, talking or napping. Phaedra led some of the visiting children about on a pony.

Lydia and another young guest were being rowed around the lake by Mr Hale, the handsome curate. She seemed to be having a good time, laughing at Mr Hale's jokes and blushing, so Catalina was happy to spend an hour walking with Lord Harry's wife.

Elena had obviously suffered a great deal in the wars in their homeland. Like Catalina she had lost her home and family and was trying to make a new start here. But she was very kind, with an engaging, easy manner that made Catalina feel at ease, not like a servant at the grand house. And it was very pleasant to speak Spanish again, to be with someone who understood so many things without the need of explaining a word.

It also distracted her at least a bit from thoughts of Jamie, from wondering what he had been doing since they parted and what he had been driven to in his work.

Catalina glanced from under her wide-brimmed hat at the house behind them. The windows gleamed back blankly, as if Castonbury itself watched her. He had not appeared for the picnic; Lady Phaedra merely said he had a great deal of work lately and had 'become no fun at all.' Catalina had felt a sharp pang of relief—or perhaps disappointment.

She wondered if he watched them now from behind one of those windows. Had he thought about her last night? She hadn't been able to sleep at all for thinking about *him*. The past and the present had become so tangled up, and she didn't know where to go next or what to do. What was the correct thing to do when one's husband—one's secret, dead husband—came up alive again?

Did he even remember what they had been to each other?

She had been able to read nothing in his eyes last night. He looked like her Jamie, though older and harder. His hands on her skin felt like Jamie's hands. Yet she could not find a spark of him in those blank eyes.

It frightened her, and made her wonder again what he had done in Spain.

'Mrs Moreno?' Elena said. 'Are you quite well?'

Startled, Catalina turned back to her. Elena looked concerned, and Catalina laughed reassuringly. 'Oh, yes. I must have just been dazzled by the sun for a moment.'

Elena laughed too, and they continued on their stroll around the lake. 'Enjoy it while you can. It seems as if it rains all the time here.'

'Have you been at Castonbury long?' Catalina asked.

'Not long, and we shall soon be off to Harry's next posting. I think he will miss his family, but we are ready for a new adventure.'

'You met your husband in Spain, yes?'

A soft smile touched Elena's face at the mention of her husband. She waved at him where he sat under a tree with his brother Giles, and he blew her a kiss. 'Yes. That was certainly quite an adventure, and not one I should care to repeat. Though I did find my Harry through it.'

'Why was Lord Harry in Spain? Was he in the army too?' Catalina asked.

'Yes, he was, but he was in Spain to find Jamie. Have you not heard the tale?'

So that was how Jamie had come to return home. His brother had searched him out. 'No indeed. I have only been at Castonbury a day. It sounds most intriguing.'

Elena laughed. 'It is a long tale.'

Catalina looked to see that Lydia was still on the lake with the curate and seemed to be having a very good time. None of the others appeared in any hurry to leave their sunny idyll. 'I have time. I would love to hear your story.'

Elena nodded and led them to a bench set in the shade of a nearby tree. From there they could see the softly rolling green vista of the gardens and a gleaming white stone folly tucked amid a grove of trees, and Elena told Catalina the tale of how she had been caught in the siege at Badajoz and cast off by her family and betrothed. Like Catalina, she had been cut off from her old life and searching for a new purpose when she met Harry Montague, who was on a quest to find out the truth about his brother's supposed death. Elena told her of the dangerous journey they had endured to find him, and what a shock it had been to find him alive at the end. She also relayed what she knew of Alicia Walters's own little intrigue, the lies she told and how it had affected the family. It was a sad story of terrible pain, but also of great love.

Catalina was so shocked when it was finished that she couldn't speak at all. It was a tale worthy of those novels Lydia loved so much—lost heirs, crumbling estates, spies, murders.

And a false wife exposed. Jamie's imposter wife.

'I can hardly believe it,' Catalina murmured. She slowly shook her head. She did remember Alicia Walters from Spain, but she could hardly credit the woman would do such a thing. She had been so quiet, so proper. So…English. Exactly the kind of lady Jamie might actually be expected to marry.

'I know,' Elena said. 'If I had not seen it all unfold myself I never would have believed it.'

'And you are quite sure her tale was false?' Catalina asked.

'I was there when Harry told Jamie what had been happening here in his absence. No one could have been more shocked—more angry. But he has allowed no one to pursue her since she fled. He says he will fix it all himself.'

Catalina could well credit that. Jamie had always gone quietly and steadily about his tasks, and was all the more deadly for it. She knew that better than anyone. She could almost have felt sorry for Alicia, if she was not so angry with her.

She curled her hands into fists and buried them in the folds of her skirt to keep from shouting out. The woman had used Jamie's name, used the tragedy of his death, to further her own ambitions. She had come here to his house, claiming a place that should have been Catalina's, if so many things had been different.

Catalina closed her eyes and bit back a sob. She had never wanted this place; it would have been as nothing without Jamie. She could never have belonged here, especially not without him. Yet it sounded as if for a time Alicia *had* belonged here.

'It was very hard for the duke to learn the truth,' Elena said. 'I understood he had become quite fond of the child. But now that Jamie is home again and the money troubles solved, I am sure all will be well. Everyone is eager for him to find a real wife soon. Especially Giles, I think. He never wanted to be the heir.'

Catalina laughed. If only they knew! And if only she knew what to do now. How to make it right. 'A real wife?'

'I think that may be why your Miss Westman was invited.'

'Miss Westman?' Catalina looked at Elena in astonishment. She had wondered herself if Lydia might make a match with another Montague cousin—but Jamie, the heir to the dukedom? 'Is she truly thought of as a bride for Lord Hatherton?'

'Did you not suspect? Harry is quite sure of it. No one has seen her in so long, and yet the duke insisted at the last minute that she must come,' Elena said. 'It does make a sort of sense. After all that has happened, the duke will want his heir's wife to be someone he can be sure of.'

'Lydia has a generous dowry, but not a large one,' Catalina murmured.

'That will not matter so much now that the inheritance troubles are in the past. Miss Westman is family, pretty and well-bred, well-behaved thanks to you. All of Jamie's siblings have made slightly shocking marriages, some rather more scandalous than others. But Jamie is the heir. Miss Westman will be an extremely proper match.'

Catalina looked at Lydia where she sat perched in the boat. She held her lacy parasol on her shoulder and was smiling shyly at the curate, her red-gold curls and pink cheeks so pretty in the sunlight. Lydia *was* a sweet girl, and always eager to please. As open and kind as a warm summer's day. She would never give the Montagues trouble or cause to fear more scandal. Unlike Catalina.

Yet Catalina also knew that being a duchess was no easy task, and the boisterous Montagues were no easy family. Like Jamie, they were complicated. Had she been sent here to help Lydia learn a new role? To help her be a suitable Marchioness of Hatherton?

It was so very strange she had to laugh. Could she let Jamie go to find a truly proper wife? She knew she could, that she had to. What they had in Spain had been nothing more than a dream, a wild folly. It could never have survived here with the pressures of everyday life. Lydia was truly more suited to this life in many ways. She was *English*.

Yet Catalina couldn't stop the shiver that went through her when she remembered how it felt when he touched her last night. How she couldn't quit staring at him, fearing that he would vanish again. And then she would never know the truth.

She rose from the bench and shook out her skirt. 'I should make sure Lydia comes inside soon. I understand we are to go to the Assembly Rooms in Buxton tonight, and she should rest before then.'

'Oh, yes,' Elena said brightly. 'I should see if I can persuade Harry to…take a rest as well. I have so enjoyed our talk, Mrs Moreno. I hope we can converse more soon.'

'I have enjoyed meeting you as well,' Catalina answered. It had been very educational—and given her a great deal more to think about. She turned and hurried down to the small boat dock to wait for Lydia to return to shore while Elena went to meet her husband.

Catalina saw what she had to do now. Let Jamie go to find his true wife. But how was she to do that?

And how was she to persuade her heart that it had to cease to care?

Chapter Ten

The lane leading to the Buxton Assembly Rooms was crowded with carriages, moving so slowly, inching forward, so that surely everyone for miles around was just waiting there on the road. And Catalina was sure that at least half the equipages belonged to Castonbury.

She drew her shawl closer around her shoulders and peered out of the window at the buildings creeping past. Ahead of her was the great landau bearing Lily and Giles, along with the duke and Mrs Landes-Fraser. And behind was Jamie in a dashing little new curricle. Not that she had paid any attention—except to be all too acutely aware of where he was at every minute.

A soft giggle made her turn away from the window. Lydia sat with two of the other young lady guests, whispering and laughing with them. She looked as if she was having a wonderful time, and Catalina smiled to see it. That was surely what weddings were for—to bring people together and make them happy.

Not upend their lives, as knowledge of a certain secret wedding years ago would surely do in this little world.

At last their carriage shuddered to a halt, and a footman rushed around to open the door. As Catalina stepped down to follow the girls up the front steps, she heard a soft tapping sound on the pavement behind her. She turned to see Jamie just as the light from one of the high windows fell over him.

He wore fashionable, if stark, black and white evening clothes, the only spark of colour a ruby pin at his cravat. His hair was brushed smoothly back from his face, revealing the arc of the scar on his cheek. And he was using the walking stick again.

As he moved beside her, Catalina couldn't help but wonder again what had happened to him. She ached to think he had been in pain, and she wanted more than she had ever wanted anything to reach out to him. To hold him close and take away anything he had suffered. To somehow make it right again.

Yet she seemed to be a cause of some of that pain to him, and it made her wonder again what had happened to him after they had parted in Spain. He gave her a grim smile as they moved up the shallow stone steps together, and he didn't quite meet her eyes. They were so near to each other, so close she could just reach out and brush his sleeve with her hand, but he was as far from her as he had ever been.

Still silent, they moved into the building behind the others. They left their wraps with the servants in the corridor and climbed the steps to the grand second-floor ballroom. It was a lovely space, a long room surmounted by crystal chandeliers and lined with marble columns.

But the ballroom was so crowded there didn't seem even an inch to move about, and Catalina wondered how anyone could possibly dance. Conversation rose in a roar all around her, words indistinct as friends greeted one another and jests were made and enjoyed. The musicians on a dais at one end of the room were tuning up.

The smells of various perfumes, baked meats and sweet punch hung in the air, and the room was warm with all the people packed inside it. Catalina could see Lydia's white gown a few feet ahead of her, but several people had slipped in between them and they were all caught in the crush. She was against the wall on one side, and Jamie was on the other.

She could feel his heat brush against her bare arm.

'It is not much like the dances in Spain, is it?' he said quietly near her ear.

Catalina laughed and shook her head. 'No, indeed. There is no canvas tent, and from what I can hear the music is a bit more…accomplished.'

Jamie smiled down at her, and for an instant he looked like the old Jamie, *her* Jamie. The man who had danced with her at those impromptu parties in Colonel Chambers's spacious tent. He had been such a grand dancer; he had always made her feel as if she was floating over the dance floor. As if for one moment things were not so dark and complicated.

'The fashions are perhaps a bit more *à la mode*

as well,' he said. 'Yet I must say I think I prefer that tent in Spain.'

Catalina glanced past his shoulder to see that most of the crowd around them had turned to stare at him, craning their necks to catch a glimpse of the long-lost Castonbury heir, found alive and returned amongst them. Most of the ladies were smoothing their hair or straightening their gowns as they watched him.

'Too much attention here?' she said. Jamie had never been one to seek to draw attention to himself. He had always quietly observed the world around him. He did not have to seek attention; it naturally came to him, as if all the light in every room collected only on him. And it had nothing to do with his rank, or even his handsome looks, but from that quiet strength at the core of him.

So much had changed since Spain, but that quality about him had not.

Jamie shrugged. He didn't even turn to look at the room, he just watched her. 'They are merely staring at my father. My siblings tell me he has seldom left the house these past few years. Everyone has forgot what he looks like.'

Catalina shook her head. 'You know that's not true. It's *you* they want to see again.'

'I am nothing to see. Just this blasted stick. They will tire of gossiping about me soon enough.'

She was sure that was not true, not when he had given them so much to gossip about. Coming back from the dead, an imposter wife and son, financial twists and turns, a passel of shocking marriages amongst his siblings—the scandal broth seemed bottomless. She didn't want to add to it.

But there was still so much she longed to know. What had he done in Spain? 'Jamie...' she whispered. Someone jostled her from behind and she remembered that this vast crowd was no place for confidences. She spun away from him and slipped past the knots of people to Lydia's side. Phaedra and her aunt Wilhemina were walking ahead of them, and Catalina could hear snatches of their conversation.

'It is too bad Jamie can't dance now,' Phaedra was saying. 'He used to enjoy it so much. And all the local ladies sought him out for their partners all the time.'

'Hmph,' Mrs Landes-Fraser said. 'They should count themselves lucky he does not dance with them now. He has become far too dour and silent. Not to mention not as handsome as he once was.'

Catalina's gloved hand curled into a fist as anger swept through her at those words. She had to bite her lip to keep from shouting in Jamie's defence. But could she really defend him? She didn't even know any longer.

Phaedra did it for her. 'You can hardly blame him for being silent! He nearly died in Spain, and I am sure he saw some horrible things we cannot even imagine. He is not the person he was when he left. None of us are.'

Phaedra glanced over her shoulder, past Catalina to where Jamie still stood near the wall. Catalina looked back to see that a portly, red-faced gentleman and two young ladies had him cornered, talking at him as he stared at them with a frozen expression.

'I only wish he could find someone to confide in,' Phaedra added softly. 'If I did not have my Bram, I would have gone insane sometimes.'

'Hmph,' Mrs Landes-Fraser said again. 'You would have done much better to marry higher in the world, girl. I do not understand any of you children...'

Lydia drew Catalina's attention then, pointing out a gown she liked across the room. They became separated from the others in the crowd, pressed in on all sides until Catalina managed to find them a spot near the windows where there were not quite so many people. There was a small breeze flowing from outside as well, and Catalina could watch the passing of the crowd as they flowed by.

'Oh, Mrs Moreno,' Lydia cried, her eyes shining with excitement as she looked out at the room. Catalina hadn't seen her so happy in any London ballroom. 'Isn't it pretty? And everyone so welcoming. I could stay at Castonbury for ever.'

'Miss Westman! Mrs Moreno,' a voice called out. Catalina turned to see Mr Hale pushing his way past a laughing group to find them. His smile was just as enthusiastic as Lydia's—especially when he looked at Lydia herself. 'How wonderful to see you here. Are you enjoying our local entertainments?'

'Oh, very much indeed, Mr Hale,' Lydia answered. She didn't look away from him.

'It must seem very pale in comparison to London Assembly Rooms,' he said.

'Not at all. I much prefer smaller gatherings, where one can really talk to people,' Lydia said as someone almost trod on her hem in the crowd.

'Then perhaps you would honour me with the first dance?' Mr Hale asked eagerly. 'With Mrs Moreno's permission, of course.'

'Oh, yes, please, Mrs Moreno?' Lydia begged. 'I do so long for a dance.'

'Then of course you may,' Catalina said with a smile. 'Go and enjoy yourselves.'

She watched as Lydia took Mr Hale's arm and he led her to a place in the set now forming on the dance floor. She leaned back against the window-sill to let the cool breeze brush over her shoulders and examined the rest of the room.

As the dancers found their places on the floors, some of the crowd went on to the refreshment room and the crush was not quite so great. The duke sat in a large armchair at one end of the long room, watching the gathering as if he was its king. Some of the cousins were clustered around him with shawls and plates of delicacies, but he waved them away impatiently. Phaedra was dancing with her husband, and the portly man who had cornered Jamie was strutting about the room. But she could not see Jamie.

The musicians launched into a lively tune, not quite as smooth and skilled as a fine London orchestra but very enthusiastic. Catalina found herself tapping her foot in time to the music, and remembered again those dances in Spain with Jamie. His hand on hers, his arm around her waist as they spun in circles until she was laughing and giddy…

'A glass of punch?' she heard Lily say. A gloved hand held out a glass of pale pink liquid.

Catalina laughed. 'Thank you. It is rather warm in here.' She took a sip. 'It's…'

'Sweet enough to make your jaw ache?' Lily said. 'Quite. The Buxton Assembly Rooms aren't famous for their refreshments, I fear.'

'They were much worse when I had to go with Lydia to Almack's,' Catalina said.

'Were they? I must remember never to go there, then.'

'But the music here is most enjoyable.'

'So it is. And everyone seems happy to see the duke out and about again.' Lily gestured with her glass at the line that had formed to greet the duke. 'Do you not care to dance, Mrs Moreno?'

Catalina shook her head. Her dancing days were done, since she could no longer dance with Jamie. He was the only one she had ever wanted to dance with, no matter what else happened between them. 'I have to look after Lydia.'

'I am not dancing tonight either. Giles has gone off to the card room, the wretch,' Lily said with a laugh. 'But Miss Westman does appear to be having a fine time.'

Catalina watched as Lydia skipped and turned along the line with Mr Hale. A bright smile was on her face, and Catalina realised she had never seen the girl having such fun before. 'So she is.'

'She seems very sweet.' Lily examined Catalina over the edge of her glass. 'But you seem too young to already be resigned to playing duenna, Mrs Moreno. You should enjoy yourself as well.'

'I am enjoying myself—in my way,' Catalina answered. How could she tell this kind woman, this new bride, how it felt when romance and passion were behind her? How it felt when she could see them again, shimmering and enticing just for ever out of reach?

Lily looked doubtful, but she just nodded and went on to make polite conversation about the people who passed by. She told Catalina who they all were and how they all fit into the life of the neighbourhood.

'And who is that?' Catalina asked as the portly man passed by again.

Lily wrinkled her nose. 'Sir Nathan Samuelson. A near neighbour to Castonbury. And a rather unpleasant individual, I fear. Don't converse with him if you can help it, Mrs Moreno. He would never let you free again.'

'I shall endeavour not to,' Catalina said with a laugh. 'He doesn't look like someone I should care to meet.'

'You heard of what happened lately at Castonbury?' Lily said quietly. 'With Miss Walters?'

Alicia—Jamie's false wife. 'Oh, yes.'

'Sir Nathan seemed rather friendly with her for a time, after Lady Kate turned down his offer flat. He appeared to court her, or something like that.'

'Something like that?' Catalina said, confused.

'I don't know. I am not sure of the whole tale there. But I would never trust Sir Nathan.'

Catalina watched the man as he continued on his circuit around the room, and noticed that few people actually spoke to him. Everyone said Alicia had disappeared. Did he know where she was?

A group of people swept up to offer Lily best wishes on the wedding and were soon followed by even more well-wishers. Lydia never stopped dancing after the first set, and before Catalina knew it the evening had grown late. The breeze had gone still from beyond the window and the room was close-packed and warm.

As Lydia went off to dance with another young man, Catalina's head suddenly throbbed. It had been a long day; it felt like a lifetime since she had come to Castonbury and found Jamie. Now the crowd and the noise seemed to press in around her. She couldn't be such a ninny as to faint again!

'I think I should find the ladies' withdrawing room for a moment,' she whispered to Lily.

'Of course,' Lily said quickly. 'You do look rather pale, Mrs Moreno. There are so many people here on too warm a night. I will watch Miss Westman.'

Catalina looked to where Lydia was still dancing. She didn't seem to look tired in the least. 'Thank you,' she murmured, and made her way slowly around to the ballroom doors.

In the corridor outside, she glanced around for something resembling a ladies' room but there was only more people, talking, laughing, sipping the sweet punch. She didn't see Jamie there. It seemed he had made his escape from the assembly long ago.

Then a door opened and closed behind a loud group at the end of the corridor, and Catalina had a glimpse of a garden beyond. She hurried towards the beckoning cool darkness and slipped outside.

It was not a large garden, but it was quiet as it backed onto a narrow lane and a field beyond. There were large old trees and a few neatly kept flower beds lined with pathways and benches where weary dancers could catch a breath of fresh air. Catalina breathed deeply of the cool breeze, and let the dark silence wrap around her. She could still hear the strains of music, but it was faint and almost ghostly.

There were a few couples walking and whispering together, yet Catalina felt almost alone as she made her way along one of the winding paths. The solitude revived her, and she felt her headache easing as she came to the low fence at the back of the garden.

She leaned on the gate and stared up into the night sky. It was black and soft as a length of velvet, dotted with a few sparkling, diamond-like stars. The moon was creeping higher above the horizon, a few wisps of cloud lying over its glow like dark blue lace. The smell of flowers and fresh, green growing things hung in the air, banishing the scent of too many perfumes and too much sweet punch. And Catalina saw that it was a truly lovely night.

Even lovelier, knowing Jamie was alive and under this same sky. No matter what had happened between them, she couldn't help caring about him.

There was a sudden sharp rustle from the field beyond the fence, and her heart leapt, startled. She held on to the top of the gate and peered out into the night. She had thought she was alone back here. Who would be creeping about there so late? A couple sneaking out of the dance? Someone from the town stumbling home drunk?

Or perhaps a thief?

As her eyes adjusted to the darkness, she thought she saw someone further down the narrow lane. It was a tall, thin man hovering near a wall, too far away for her to see him well. Yet somehow she sensed he was watching her. Watching—and waiting for something.

Catalina took a deep breath and stiffened her shoulders. 'Who is there?' she called out. 'Do I know you?'

The man suddenly spun around and ran away. For an instant, Catalina saw the moonlight catch on some kind of bright-coloured hair and then he was gone.

She knew she should go back inside, but her heart was still pounding. She didn't like the feeling seeing that figure left behind.

'Talking to someone, Catalina?' a man said, and she whirled around with her fists raised— only to see that it was Jamie who stood behind her.

'You startled me,' she gasped. 'You move far too quietly.'

He gave her a wry smile. 'My apologies. I will

be sure to beat my stick against the trees next time. Are you alone out here?'

Catalina glanced back down the lane. The spot where the man had been was quite empty.

Feeling foolish, she hurried around the nearest tree and leaned back to let its solid trunk hold her up. It had been such a strange, dizzying time, she hardly knew what to say or think, how to behave. Her confusion only grew when Jamie followed her and stood close to her in the night.

She reached up, compelled to touch his face, to ease the tense lines on his brow with her fingertips. How well she remembered the feel of him under her touch! The skin smooth as taut satin over his sharp cheekbones, the roughness of the evening whiskers over his hard jaw. The new scar that arced along his cheek. He was close to her now, so close she could drown in the grey sky of his eyes.

She curled her fingers around his face and just looked and looked at him. *Jamie, Jamie.*

He, too, seemed enchanted by this moment out of time, woven out of the past and the magical attraction that still bound them together. Jamie caught her hand in his and turned his face to press a kiss in the cup of her palm. His lips were so soft and firm at the same time, so gentle where they touched her skin.

'Catalina,' he said hoarsely. His voice echoed against her hand and seemed to move through her whole body, right to her very heart. 'I've missed you.'

His other hand slid around the nape of her neck, just under the loose knot of her hair, and he drew her even closer. So very close.

Catalina knew she should pull away from him, that this should not be happening. But she could no more leave him than she could cease to breathe. She craved Jamie's kiss—she *needed* it. She had been so long without him.

Jamie's movements were slow and gentle, giving her time to draw back from him—or to learn him again. As her eyes closed and she leaned into him, she felt the warmth of his breath on her cheeks, the heat of his body against hers, the clean, wondrously familiar scent of him. She twined her arms around his neck to bring him even closer to her. She felt the short, soft strands of his hair cling to her gloves and she went up on tiptoe as she held on to him.

Their lips met softly once, twice, as if they were slowly finding their way back to each other. Then temptation and heat rose between them as memories burst free, and Catalina couldn't resist another second. Their mouths melded in a blurry, hot rush, and she felt his tongue seeking hers, tracing the soft seam of her lips before sliding inside.

'Mmm.' Catalina sighed at the taste of him. So dark and rich and just as perfect as she remembered. The smoothness of sweet brandy overlaying something more enticing and dangerous, something that was only him. She held on to him tightly and traced her tongue over his.

Jamie groaned and his arms closed hard around her. He drew her up against him until their bodies were as close as layers of silk and wool allowed them to be. But Catalina wanted to be even closer.

She slid one hand along the side of his throat and traced her fingertips over his chest. She could feel his strength through the crisp linen of his cravat and the smooth brocade of his waistcoat. She felt the small bump of her ring on its chain, and his heart leapt under her palm. A rush of joy went through her at the feel of its rhythm—it meant he was *alive*, that his heart at least still responded to hers even though their lives were separate now.

Then everything around her went soft and dark, and she was utterly lost in the kiss. Jamie's kiss, his touch, had become the beginning and the end of the whole world, all she knew and wanted.

His lips slid away from hers and trailed over her cheek to press the tender spot just behind her ear. His breath brushed over her skin and she shivered. 'Jamie,' she whispered, clinging to him as the ground seemed to rock beneath them.

'Say that again,' he whispered as his fingertips softly brushed the underside of her breast through her grey silk gown. 'Damn, your voice, Catalina—I've never heard anything like it.'

'Jamie, I…' she began, but her whispers and the harsh sound of his breath were cut off by a burst of laughter from further in the garden. Real life intruding on them yet again.

Catalina's eyes flew open and she stumbled back from Jamie. His arms fell away from her and he stared at her with burning bright eyes. For an instant his cold, distant mask had dropped and she saw her own desire reflected in the raw agony on his handsome face.

But then he stepped back as well, and that smooth facade dropped back over him. It was as if he vanished from her all over again. Bitter disappointment flooded coldly through her veins, drowning out all the burning delight of rediscovering something that had once been so magical.

He ran his hand roughly through his hair and he stared at her as if he had never seen her before. 'Catalina,' he said, his voice low and harsh. 'I am sorry—I don't know what came over me. Old memories, perhaps.'

Old memories. Catalina nodded sadly. That was all that was left for them now, surely that was what Jamie was saying. 'No. There is nothing to be sorry about, Jamie. Tonight was only an old dream of Spain, yes? It will vanish in the light. We will be as we are now. You don't—you needn't worry about me. I understand how things are for you. And I will never tell anyone what happened. As far as I am concerned, you are free.'

Jamie gave his head a fierce shake and opened his mouth as if he would say something more. As if he would argue or, even worse, apologise again. She couldn't bear it if he regretted that perfect kiss along with everything else.

'Just a dream,' she repeated quickly. She gave him one more smile and whirled around to hurry from the garden as fast as her shaking legs could carry her. The laughing group that had emerged from the Assembly Rooms didn't even notice her and she slipped past them into the corridor. She didn't stop, and she didn't—couldn't—look back.

It wasn't until later that she realised she had lost her shawl.

Jamie stood in the garden for long moments after Catalina left, letting the cool evening breeze wash over him. He was still not fit for polite society, for assemblies and dinners, polite conversation and manners. He should hide away in a quiet room, like a wounded bear, or he would only do such things as grab women and kiss them in public gardens.

No—not just any woman. Catalina.

He had only meant to speak to her, to find out what she was watching so intently out on the street, but as soon as he touched her it had had to be more. He'd had to do more.

Despite everything that had happened, all the complications of their past, the fact that she seemed to want nothing more than to forget him, he wanted her. The sparks that had ignited between them the first time they'd met were still there, binding them together. She drove him mad, as no other woman had ever done. And the taste of her kiss…

'Blast it all,' Jamie cursed, and turned away from the garden. As he looked back to the building, he glimpsed a length of pale fabric on the ground. Catalina's shawl.

He bent to pick it up, and a hint of her sweet perfume rose from the soft folds. She would surely be missing it later, in the chilly rooms of Castonbury.

He had to return it to her—and to find out what she had been looking at out here that had startled her so.…

Chapter Eleven

Meet me in the garden folly at midnight, Catalina,
I beg you. I must talk to you. J.

Catalina stared down at the note in her hand, which had been slipped under her door soon after they returned from the Assembly Rooms. Jamie's bold, slashing black handwriting stood out in the candlelight, luring her to follow its words.

She sighed and looked out of her chamber window. She couldn't see the folly but she knew it was out there, waiting for her. Those brief words and that one kiss between them could not be the end. She knew that. There was too much between her and Jamie to be so easily finished.

She had to meet him. There was so much unsaid between them, so much she didn't understand.

She picked up the shawl that had been handed to her by one of the footmen as she left the Assembly Rooms, the same shawl she had lost in the garden. The soft cashmere folds were cool, but she imagined she could smell the lingering essence of his cologne there. She quickly wrapped it around her shoulders and slipped out of the bedroom door.

The house was empty and silent, everyone tucked up in their own chambers for the night. No light shone beneath Lydia's door, so Catalina hoped the girl had gone to sleep without staying up to read her horrid novels. The corridor was lit only by a few flickering sconces, which seemed to make the portraits on the walls peer down at her disapprovingly as she slipped past.

Catalina ran down the stairs and out the front doors, praying the heavy wood wouldn't slam behind her. The wind had died down, leaving the night still and silent. She followed the glow of the moon to the gardens and along the pathway that led to the folly. It glowed a mellow, pure white in the darkness.

She tiptoed up the shallow stone steps and past the pillars into the small, cool, domed space. A statue of Cupid holding his bow aloft stood in the middle of the round room, and for a moment she feared he was the only one there. Her heart sank and she suddenly felt so very alone.

But then Jamie appeared from the shadows and her heart soared again. He had shed his coat and his waistcoat was unfastened, revealing the bright white linen of his shirt, the loops of his loose cravat. He was surely the most beautiful sight she had ever seen, like a god of the night.

'Catalina,' he said, and his voice was rough with some hidden emotion. He moved slowly closer to her, his booted footsteps echoing in the carved dome above them. 'You came.'

'I—of course I did,' she whispered. She couldn't stay away, not from him.

And suddenly his arms slid around her, drawing her tight against him as she clutched at his shoulders.

'How I've missed you,' he said. 'What you said at the Assembly Rooms—it can't be the end for us. Not when the truth of so much lies between us.'

Catalina shook her head and bit back a sob. She had thought the same thing, yet how could they speak rationally when simply being near him made her feel so much? He freed so very many emotions and passions that she had hidden and denied for so long. Ever since she had lost him.

Losing him once had nearly destroyed her. How could she bear it again?

Jamie seemed to sense all those things she couldn't say, for he pulled her even closer, and his mouth came down on hers. He didn't rush or push her; he wasn't harsh with her, that had never been Jamie's way. But his mouth opened over hers, his tongue tracing her lips as he sought to quench his burning desire for her. Catalina opened to him, letting him in. Her body remembered his kiss at the Assembly Rooms and craved yet more and more.

Yes—*this* was what she had longed for, the sensation of every rational thought flying out of her and falling down into pure, burning need. Just as Jamie had always made her do.

His hand slid down her back as he deepened the kiss, and the shawl he had wrapped around her fell away from her shoulders. The night air washed over her, but she only felt it for an instant before it was replaced by the heat of his touch.

His hands slid under the curve of her hips and he lifted her up high against his body. He swung her around until she was braced against the low marble banister that ran around the folly. She clasped her knees to either side of his lean hips and arched into his body.

His lips slid over her cheek and down her neck as she arched her head back, his tongue swirling lightly in the hollow at the base of her neck where her pulse pounded out a frantic beat. It had always felt like this when he touched her, as if something dark and secret deep inside of her reached out to the darkness in him.

She felt his palm slide up from her waist to lightly cup her breast, stroking it through her thin gown.

'Blast it all, Catalina,' he growled. 'I need— need…'

'I know,' she gasped as his touch slid over her. She twined her fingers in his hair and drew his kiss back to the soft curve of her neck. She trembled as his warm breath washed over her skin and cried out when his hand closed hard over her breast.

'I don't want to still need you like this,' he said roughly.

'I don't want to need you either. I worked so very hard to forget you.' To forget what he had done.

'Did you forget me?'

Catalina shook her head. She closed her eyes tightly, shutting out the rest of the world so she could revel in the bright pleasure of knowing his touch again. 'I never could.'

'I never forgot you either. Never, Catalina.'

He tugged down her light silk bodice and chemise, baring her breast to the moonlight. Catalina bit back a sob as he rubbed the roughened pad of his thumb over her nipple. It hardened and ached under his caress.

'You're still so beautiful,' he said. She opened her eyes to watch, mesmerised, as he bent his head and took her nipple into his mouth, his tongue swirling around it lightly until she couldn't breathe. Her legs tightened around his waist and she pulled him closer into the curve of her body.

He drew her deeper into the hot wetness of his mouth, biting down lightly and then soothing it with the edge of his tongue. She heard the mingling of their breath, harsh and uneven, the swirl of the wind around the marble walls, the lapping of the water from the lake along the shore. But none of it mattered. Only Jamie, his mouth, his hands, his body against hers. Just him.

His hand traced along her bent leg until he caught the hem of her skirt in his fist. He drew it up and up, over her bare skin until he traced the soft curve just where her hip met her thigh. Catalina was suddenly glad there hadn't been time to put her stockings back on.

Then she felt his fingers move even lower. He nudged her thighs wider and traced his thumb along her damp folds. She cried out his name as he slid his touch inside her and pressed deep.

'Jamie,' she sobbed, and his open mouth came over hers to catch her words.

She reached out for him desperately, her hand flattening over his chest where she felt the pounding of his heart. She slid her touch down, down, over his flat stomach, the sharp angle of his hip. At last she covered that hardness in his breeches and closed her fingers around him in the way she remembered he liked so much.

He groaned deeply as she moved her hand down and up again, harder, faster.

'Are you trying to kill me?' he said.

Catalina laughed and wrapped her legs even tighter around him. 'Do you not like that now? You certainly used to.'

'I like it too well. That's the problem.' Jamie's hand slid away from her, slowly trailing along her leg as if he couldn't quite let her go. But he gently lowered her to her feet and her hand fell away from him. He braced his palms to the marble railing on either side of her, not touching her. But she could feel him shaking just as she was.

On trembling legs, Catalina moved away from him and sat down on one of the stone benches that lined the folly. She braced her palms on her legs and dragged in a shuddering breath.

'I should go back soon,' she said. 'It grows very late.'

Jamie nodded brusquely. He sat down beside her, close but not touching, as the darkness closed in around them again.

'I am sorry, Catalina,' he said. 'I didn't ask you to meet me here so I could grab you like that.'

Catalina laughed. 'Obviously I did not mind it so much.'

Jamie laughed too, and leaned his head back against the wall as he stared up into the dome of the folly. 'Neither did I. That has not changed between us.'

'No,' she said quietly. 'It's just everything else that has changed.'

He was quiet for a long moment. 'And some things will never change.'

Like his family? His duty? 'Why did you ask me to meet you here, Jamie?' she asked.

'Only this,' he said. 'To tell you that you were right.'

Puzzled, Catalina examined his expressionless face in the shadows. 'Right about what?'

'About Spain, the Bourbons.'

Catalina went very still and stared at him in the moonlight. She remembered their old quarrels, the memory of what had happened to her country under the iron fist of King Ferdinand. How she could never go back there. And Jamie was a part of that.

Jamie nodded as if he could read her thoughts. 'I thought I was doing my duty, that I was doing what needed to be done for the security of all Europe. But in the end I left my family, my first duty, in dire straits while I worked to help re-establish a vengeful madman to the throne. There are times I can't even look at myself in the mirror knowing what has happened. Especially...'

'Especially what?' Catalina whispered.

'Especially when I thought I had lost you and I couldn't say these things to you. That you were right. That I am sorry. Sorry for so many things.'

Catalina shook her head. She closed her eyes tightly against the tears that prickled at her eyes. It was all too, too late. Everything. 'We have both paid for our mistakes now. We've done what we had to do and now we must go forward. You are here with your family now, and they seem so happy to have you back.'

'And you, Catalina?'

She laughed. 'I am glad you are here, too. When I thought you were dead...' Her heart had been torn out. But she had somehow gone on living. She could surely do that again.

'That was one of the reasons I was able to accept my task,' Jamie said quietly. 'When you were gone it hardly mattered to me what happened.'

A tiny spark of hope bloomed in Catalina's heart, but she knew it was futile. That had been a long time ago, and so much had changed. But knowing that he *had* missed her—it was something she could cling to. One certain thing in the midst of so much that was confusing.

'I meant what I said earlier, Jamie,' she said. 'You must consider yourself free of me. You have to do what your family needs now.' Catalina despaired of knowing how she could let him go— divorce was too public, and a scandal was the last thing his family needed. But she had to do what was best for him.

'Do I?' Jamie shook his head, that unreadable little half-smile touching his lips. He looked towards the darkened house, and Catalina glanced over to see that a golden light glowed in one of the upstairs windows. Soon other people would be awake, and she needed to be safely in her chamber before they were.

She stood up and tightened her shawl around her shoulders as she turned away from Jamie. 'You know you do. And now I must go.'

She wanted to leave quickly, to get away from the folly without looking at him again. He was too good at reading people; he would see her confusion and pain right away, and her attempt to do what was right would be painfully prolonged.

He didn't say anything, he didn't try to hold her back, but his hand brushed over hers as she swept past him.

'Sleep well, Catalina,' he called softly as she slipped out into the garden. 'But remember—this isn't over yet.'

Catalina ran back to the house, not stopping until her chamber door was safely shut behind her. She feared that he was too right—it wasn't over, at least not in her heart. And it never would be.

Chapter Twelve

Buxton was crowded and noisy as Jamie eased his curricle past a large, lumbering landau and turned down a side lane. Shop doors were thrown open for the customers who hurried in and out laden with packages, calling out to friends, finishing the morning's errands. It was a warm day despite the heavy grey skies that threatened rain later and the damp air, and everyone wanted to be home before the storm came.

No one paid him any attention as he made his way through the town. He wore a plain grey coat and a broad-brimmed hat drawn low over his brow, and no one seemed to recognise the carriage. He liked those few moments of solitude, where there was only the horse and the road, and no one in his family there to watch him with ill-concealed concern in their eyes.

They never asked him questions, but he could tell they wanted to know what had really happened. One day he would have to tell them, but not yet. Not while he still had no words for the guilt that twisted at him when he thought of how he had left them, of the pain he had caused.

Not when the issue of Catalina was still unresolved. His wife.

She said she considered him free of her, that he had to do his duty to his family now. Yet what of his duty to her? He had to do what was right, but how could he when she would not let him? If she would not let him be her husband, he still had to take care of her.

And he had to start doing right by her and his family by settling old scores. As he had worked on the estate in the past few days after the assembly, he had thought about it all a great deal.

Jamie drew up at a small house set on a quiet street not far from the Assembly Rooms and climbed down from the high carriage seat. There was no one else passing by this row of small but respectable dwellings; it was far from the shops and the more fashionable neighbourhoods. The houses were plain and well-kept, quite unexceptional in every way. There were only a few shops across the street that catered mostly to the comfortably off merchants, widows and lawyers who lived in the houses.

And that made it the perfect place for someone to hide in plain sight.

Jamie knocked on the black-painted door at the top of a small set of stone steps, and it was quickly opened.

'You are early,' Alicia said as he bowed over her hand before slipping inside. 'Crispin is taking his nap and the maid has gone out on an errand.'

'Are you both comfortable here, Miss Walters?' Jamie asked. He left his hat on a small bench in the hall and followed her into the tidy sitting room. A fire burned in the grate against the damp day, and an open work box sat on the table, spilling out colourful embroidery silks next to a tea set. A few toys were scattered across the floor.

'Oh, yes, very comfortable,' Alicia said as she scooped up the toys and deposited them in their box. 'It was so kind of you to find this place for us. I certainly do not deserve it after…well, after everything.'

Jamie shook his head. 'You have surely been punished enough for your mistakes. I am still paying for mine.'

Alicia gave him a puzzled glance. 'Whatever do you mean, Lord Hatherton? What mistakes could you possibly have made?'

He smiled. 'Nothing to worry about at the moment, Miss Walters. How is young Crispin settling in?'

'Very well indeed. Though I think this street is a bit quiet for him. He does like to watch the horses go by.' Alicia poured out two cups of tea. 'I know I have no right to ask, but how is everyone at Castonbury? How is…'

She broke off, and a faint blush touched her pale cheeks.

Jamie sat down by the fire and took the cup she offered him. 'How is Mr Everett?'

Alicia bit her lip. 'How—how did you know?'

Jamie shrugged. 'He has often expressed concern about you. He is a good man.'

'A good man I do not deserve.' Alicia sat down across from him and stared down into her cup.

'Have you discovered where Captain Webster is hiding yet?'

'Not at present, but he cannot stay hidden for ever. Have you had word from him?'

Alicia shook her head. 'I left him a message in our old hiding place telling him where I am and offering to share a new scheme with him, just as you instructed. He has not yet replied.' She gave a small frown. 'But I think I saw him a few nights ago.'

Jamie's senses sharpened. 'Saw him where?'

'In the lane behind the house, just past the garden that backs onto the Assembly Rooms. I was putting Crispin to bed in the nursery and happened to glance out the window. I thought I saw a man with red hair, but then he was gone so fast. I could have only imagined it.'

Jamie didn't like the thought of Webster lurking about like a phantom, even if it was all part of the plan to draw him out. 'You should let me set guards on the house, as I suggested before.'

'No,' Alicia said adamantly. 'I don't want to scare Crispin. And no one should know where we are. We have the maid, and she does seem to notice everything that happens in the kitchen and out on the street. She loves to tell me all about it.'

'Then at least you must send me word immediately if you even suspect you see Webster again,' Jamie said.

Alicia nodded. 'Of course I will. I want him found as much as you do. That is the only way I can go on with my life. Whatever that may be.'

Jamie knew all too well how that felt. Life felt as if it was at a standstill until he could catch Webster and restore his family's home and honour. Only then could he somehow move forward.

He and Alicia made more plans for trying to track down Webster and he left as the day moved into late afternoon. A few raindrops were falling from the sky as he drove out of town and turned back towards Castonbury. In the distance he glimpsed a figure hurrying along the side of the road, a slender woman in a blue dress and jacket. Her back was to him, her head bent, but Jamie could tell even from that distance that it was Catalina.

He urged the horse faster as the rain began to fall thicker and heavier. He came alongside her just as she stumbled in the mud. He leapt down from the carriage and ignored the twinge in his own leg to catch her as she fell.

'Catalina?' he shouted over the rain. 'Where are you going? What are you doing here?'

She looked up at him, raindrops glistening on her lashes, and he was shocked to see the raw hurt in her eyes. It flashed there for only a second before she looked away, but he wanted more than he had ever wanted anything to take it away.

But first he had to get her out of this cursed rain.

Chapter Thirteen

Jamie was with Alicia Walters.

Catalina hurried as fast as she could down the lane, not even seeing where she was going as she tried to get away from Buxton and from that house. She hadn't felt the first drops of rain at all.

The day had started in such an ordinary fashion. Lydia was working on some amateur theatricals with the other young guests, watched over by Lily, but they had needed some new fabric for costumes and Catalina had volunteered to go and fetch it. Phaedra was going a few farms over to look at some horses for sale, and had offered to drop Catalina in Buxton if she wanted to buy the fabric there and do some extra shopping. It had seemed like a fine idea, a chance to be alone and think in quiet. She had planned to walk back to

Castonbury when she was done and get some exercise as well.

But then she had turned down that quiet street of small houses. When she had glimpsed Jamie there, so surprising and sudden, at first she had felt a rush of gladness. She had just raised her hand to wave to him when the door had opened and Alicia Walters had appeared there. Alicia, who everyone thought had run away after her crime was discovered. Yet she seemed to have been expecting Jamie.

And Catalina had been able to do nothing but rush off, forgetting even the errand that had brought her to town in the first place. She found herself now on the country road and couldn't even really remember getting there.

The sky had burst open and dropped the heavy burden of rain onto the earth, as it had been threatening to do all day. Catalina hadn't even noticed the first chilly drops, she had been so lost in the memory of Jamie holding Alicia's hand, walking with her into that house. She had been lost in that terrible sense of feeling so foolish.

But she hadn't been able to escape the rain for long. The drops had quickly become a deluge, cold and needle-sharp, pounding against her head and soaking through her spencer and dress. She had stumbled in a muddy hole and her half-boot had almost been sucked from her foot.

'*Maldición,*' she had cursed, and wrenched herself free. She had dragged her ruined straw bonnet from her head and turned her face up to the angry heavens. The storm seemed to reflect all her anger and confusion back at her.

'Catalina! What are you doing, you foolish woman?' she heard someone shout over the roar of the rain.

Jamie. It was Jamie who had followed her from the town. Catalina laughed and covered her face with her dripping hands. She felt his strong arms around her waist as he lifted her free of the mud hole.

'Catalina, where are you going?' he asked roughly, setting her back on her feet. 'What are you doing here?'

Catalina shook her head. What was *he* doing here? What was he doing visiting a woman who had deceived his entire family? A woman no one had seen in weeks? Had they all been wrong about Alicia and her relationship with Jamie? 'I was shopping,' she said. When she had set out that morning on her errand it had seemed like such an ordinary day. How long ago that was.

The cold seemed to have seeped deep into her skin now, and she shivered.

'Shopping?' Jamie said. 'Did you drop your parcels somewhere?'

'No, I bought nothing,' Catalina answered. 'But you—what were you doing there? You said you were looking into a land purchase.'

Would he tell her about meeting Alicia? About what he was really doing with her? He stared down at her for a long moment, his eyes again so flat and still, so unreadable. She thought for an instant he might answer her, but then he just shook his head and gave her a crooked little smile.

'We need you inside this very minute, before you catch the ague,' he said. 'It would be terrible if you missed the wedding festivities.'

Before she knew what he was doing, he bent and caught her under her knees to swing her up into his arms. She was so surprised by his sudden movement, and still so confused by the burst of cold rain and seeing him with Alicia, that she didn't make a protest. Jamie's body was so warm and alive under the wet layers of their clothes, she just wanted to curl close to him. So close she could disappear inside his heat and never be seen again.

'Back to Castonbury?' she murmured as he put her on his carriage seat and climbed up beside her.

'Too far,' he said. He led the horse onto a twisting pathway off the lane she hadn't noticed before. When they could go no further, he tied up the horse under the shelter of a large tree and lifted her down again. She saw that he was limping a bit, his steps uneven on the muddy ground.

'Put me down now,' she insisted. 'I can walk.'

'In those ruined shoes? Certainly not. Now be still, woman, or you'll tumble us both into the mud.'

His arms tightened around her, and one look at his grimly determined face kept her silent. She let her head fall to his shoulder and just held on to him as he carried her.

'There is a shelter of sorts in those trees not far from here,' Jamie said. 'They once used it in sheep-shearing season, if it's still there. Not grand, but you can get warm there.'

They walked on in silence, until they found that the shelter was indeed still there. It was a simple, square structure of weathered stone with pens outside for the sheep. There were no windows, but there was a chimney and even a small pile of firewood under a box. Jamie shoved open the rickety door with his shoulder and stepped inside.

For a moment the sudden silence after the rain was deafening. The drops pattered softly on the old roof, but it was dry in the room.

'It's not much,' Jamie said as he lowered her to her feet. 'But it's home for now. Can you stand?'

'Yes, of course,' Catalina said, trying not to let her teeth chatter. She leaned against the closed door as Jamie went to kneel by the stone hearth. It *wasn't* much, just a small room with no furniture that smelled faintly of sheep, but it looked like a miraculous haven to her. Shelves rose up one wall, holding stacks of woollen blankets and pottery jugs.

Catalina shivered and wrapped her arms around herself as she watched Jamie coax the first faint embers of the fire into real flames. They leapt higher, casting his damp skin and hair into a celestial golden light.

She remembered how he had bowed over Alicia's hand, how well they had looked together, and she wondered again what he had been doing there. What was really going on in his life? Had she ever really known him?

Soon the fire was full of roaring life, the orange flames leaping high, cracking and snapping. Sweet-acrid smoke tinged the scent of the cold, damp air, curling around her as if it would draw her away from the door. Jamie looked at her over his shoulder. He didn't smile now; his expression was strangely still and grim.

He ran his hands through his wet hair and pushed the strands straight back from his face. The light danced over the angles of his aristocratic features, the sharpness of his cheekbones and nose, the strong line of his jaw. The scar on his cheek. He looked so austere in that flickering light, like a medieval monk or king. Austere and beautiful.

Her heart ached with it.

Catalina shivered again, and he pushed himself to his feet. As she watched he crossed the room to get a blanket from the shelf. He came back to her to tuck the rough wool around her shoulders. 'You should come and sit by the fire,' he said quietly.

She let him slip his arm around her shoulders and lead her to the warm, welcoming circle of the blaze. He laid another blanket down on the rough floor for her to sit on.

'You're still shivering,' he said.

Catalina nodded. She was shaking—but not just from the rain. He was so near to her she was dizzy with it, longing to reach out and touch him, to feel the strong warm reality of him and know again that he was no dream.

Jamie knelt beside her with a muttered oath and reached under her muddy hem for her foot. He placed it against his thigh and deftly slipped the buttons of her ruined boot from the stiffened leather.

'Your clothes are wet through,' he said, not looking up at her as he removed her other boot. 'You should take them off and wrap up in more of those blankets. You'll never get warm otherwise.'

Take off her clothes? Be *naked* with him? Catalina almost laughed aloud hysterically. What sort of insane things would happen then, if she felt this way when he just touched her foot? It didn't seem like a sensible idea.

Of course it wasn't as if he had never seen her unclothed before. He had taken off her clothes, kissed every inch of the skin he had bared....

Catalina shivered again. She turned her head to stare into the flames. 'What of you?' she whispered. 'You are also soaked through, Jamie.'

'I'm used to it,' he said.

'I don't care if you *are* used to it. I would hate it if you caught a cold and missed your brother's wedding festivities because you chased me down in the rain,' she said. He shook his head, and she raised her hand in a gesture that said she would brook no arguments. 'I insist. We should both get out of our garments. It seems so foolish to sit here in them when we are both adults who have seen so much of the world. I will even turn my back—very proper.'

Jamie burst out laughing. Catalina had never heard him laugh like that before, full out, nothing held back. It was a rich, glowing sound, brighter and deeper than any spiced wine on a cold night. It made Catalina feel warmer just hearing it, and she found herself actually giggling with him.

'Oh, yes,' he gasped. 'Very proper indeed.' He sat back on his heels and braced his palms on his thighs as he laughed. 'As if I don't remember what you look like naked, Catalina. Your beautiful skin, the curve of your back. Do you still have that little freckle just behind...'

'Stop!' Catalina cried. Her sides ached from laughing. She wrapped her arms around her waist and shook her head, trying to catch her breath.

Finally they were able to stop laughing, and somehow the tense atmosphere in the little room felt easier, lighter. Jamie leaned forward and rested his hands on the blanket on either side of her hips. He was so close she could smell the rain on his skin and see the drops of it sparkling in his hair.

'When did we become so ridiculous, Catalina?' he said. 'So silly and prudish.'

'I am not prudish,' Catalina protested. 'Of course I know we have seen each other before. I just think we should be...'

Naked together again? Kissing, touching? Yes, all of those things—if only it was not all too late.

'Should be what?' he said.

'Cautious,' she answered, far more firmly than she felt.

He studied her for a long, tense moment. Finally he nodded and pushed himself to his feet.

'Fair enough,' he said. He turned to face the corner, his arms crossed over his chest. 'There now, my back is turned.'

Catalina slowly stood up and stepped closer to the fire, her own back turned to him. She unbuttoned and removed her spencer to spread it out on the hearth. She could hear nothing from Jamie except the soft sound of his breath mingled with the patter of rain on the walls outside. She eased the long sleeves of her dress down her arms, pulling at the high, gathered neckline until the wet, clinging muslin fell away. The fabric slithered down to a sodden pile at her feet until she stood in only her chemise and stockings. Her damp skin, bared to the warm air, prickled.

'Now you,' she said. After a long moment she heard the slide and rustle of Jamie's clothes as he undressed. She closed her eyes tightly, but in that darkness it was even worse. She could see it all in her mind—that wet shirt falling away from Jamie's chest, leaving him bare. The smooth, warm skin, the strong muscles of his chest and his shoulders flexing with his movement. His long, elegant hands loosening the front of his breeches, easing them away from his lean hips—oh, yes, she remembered it all. She could just imagine those breeches moving lower and lower....

Catalina groaned and pressed her hands over her closed eyes. Jamie was right—they were ridiculous. It had been so long; she shouldn't still want him this much.

'Catalina, are you all right?' Jamie said. She heard a soft whisper of sound, his footsteps on the floor, a rustle of cloth, and then a warm, dry blanket eased over her shoulders.

'You're still shaking,' he said, so quiet and deep.

Catalina swallowed hard and nodded. 'The rain. When do you think it will end?'

'Very soon. Don't worry—I'm sure your charge, Miss Westman, is safe enough at Castonbury with my sister.' Jamie stepped away from her, and Catalina opened her eyes to see that he knelt down to stir at the fire. 'Come, sit closer, it will warm you.'

Under the shelter of the blanket, Catalina wriggled out of the chemise and unfastened the velvet garters to roll down her damp stockings. Now she had only the blanket over her nakedness—and Jamie still wore his breeches. All her wild imaginings were for naught.

Catalina almost laughed and she clapped her hand over her mouth. The other hand held her blanket closed at her throat.

'Come, sit,' Jamie said again. He pulled the blankets on the floor closer to the hearth.

'I know Miss Westman is fine at Castonbury,' Catalina said as she sat down. She tucked her legs up under her and watched the fire leap higher. 'Your family has been very kind to her.'

'They can be kind sometimes,' Jamie said with a laugh. 'We're not always complete savages, no matter what the gossip says about us.'

They could be kind when they had a purpose? Was that how Jamie truly thought? Was that what had happened in Spain? Catalina blurted out, 'They want you to marry her, you know.'

Jamie turned his head to look at her, that half-smile on his lips. Half his face was lit by the fire and half cast in shadows. 'My father thinks I should. He considers her very suitable.'

'And you?'

'How can I marry her, Catalina, when I am married to you?'

And there it was, said aloud at last. They were married. What were they to do about it? The words seemed to hover in the air between them, filling the tiny building.

Catalina tightened her fist around the blanket. 'We aren't really. I would never stand in the way of your life here.'

'How could you not? Do you not remember Spain?'

'Of course I remember.' Catalina closed her eyes. She remembered it all, every moment with him. But that was so long ago, when they were different people. 'But it's all changed since then. I see that so clearly since I came to Castonbury. You need a wife who can be a part of that, as I'm sure Lydia could. There must be a way we could make it so.'

Jamie was quiet for a long moment. 'You think I should marry Miss Westman?'

'I think you must do what your family thinks is right,' Catalina said, even as her heart ached to say the words. She wanted to cry out that *no*, she did not want him to marry Lydia! But she had been brought up the strict Spanish way, and that included doing the dutiful thing even when it was difficult. 'I am sure our marriage cannot be legal here in England. It was such a rushed affair, and the chaplain is dead now. There is no one to remember it at all.'

'No one but us,' Jamie said quietly.

'Yes. No one but us.' Catalina turned to look at him. Her beautiful, brave, dashing Jamie. How she had missed him. How she missed him still, despite everything that was between them now. Family, duty. Alicia Walters. Everything that had happened in Spain.

'Perhaps there is someone you prefer to Lydia,' she said.

'Oh? And who would that be? Which of the oh-so-many candidates for my hand would you recommend?' he said wryly.

Catalina thought of Alicia's hand on his arm, his smile as he looked down at her and stepped into the house. 'Perhaps Miss Walters, now that she seems to have reappeared. I hear she did fit in very well at Castonbury.'

Jamie's eyes widened in surprise. 'Alicia?'

'I saw you with her in town.'

He gave a humourless laugh. 'Surely you know the tale of her tenure there at Castonbury?'

'Yes, I have heard something of it.'

'Then you know she could never go back there.'

'You don't seem angry with her,' Catalina said.

Jamie shrugged, staring back into the fire. 'I know that sometimes people do terrible things for what they suppose are the best of reasons.'

As he had done? Catalina longed to pull him around to face her, to break down that brittle facade that always seemed to enclose him now and demand he tell her exactly what he meant. That he tell her *everything*. But she feared he would turn away from her, close himself off for ever, as he had in Spain when he had told her only part of his work there.

'I won't marry Alicia,' he said. He said nothing about Lydia. 'She is assisting me with something, and then she will go away from here.'

'And what will you do?'

'I have no idea, Catalina,' he said with another of those hollow laughs. 'Right now I just want to sit here with you and listen to the rain, and forget.'

Catalina wanted that too. Just to be with Jamie,

here in this strange little place. This small moment out of real time, just the two of them as it had once been.

She tucked a folded blanket behind her head as a pillow and slid down into the warm nest. Jamie laid his hand on her bare foot as it peeked from the hem of the blanket, and for a long time there was no sound between them, just the rain and the snap of the fire. The moments spread out like a wide river, slowly flowing between them with no beginning or end.

As the fire burned down, Jamie leaned forward to stir it to life again. The blanket wrapped around his torso slipped off one muscled shoulder and revealed to the light a delicate, terrible tracery of pale pink scars that echoed the one on his cheek.

Catalina felt like she couldn't breathe at the sight of them. She wanted so much to lean closer to him, to press her lips to those scars. She ached to think how he must have suffered, and she wished that her kiss could erase those marks and make her life whole again.

Make both their lives whole again.

But she knew that wasn't possible. She leaned

back against the blankets and stared again into the fire. She listened to the lash of the rain and let the warmth of the smoke, the clean scent of Jamie's cologne, wrap around her as he lay down beside her.

'Tell me a story,' she said, remembering how he had once told her tales of English knights and chivalry on the long, hot nights in Spain, and how she would tell him Spanish tales in return.

Jamie laughed. 'I don't know any good tales I have not already told you. Not like you and the adventures of Don Quixote.'

'I remember your stories of King Arthur. But I also liked your stories of Castonbury and your family,' Catalina said. 'It didn't sound like a real place at all but a fairyland.'

Jamie was quiet for a long moment. 'It seemed like a fairyland to me too, when I was in Spain for so long. But I told you everything then. I have nothing new.'

'Did you?'

'Yes indeed. You know of the pranks my siblings and I pulled, about my mother and what it was like when she was gone. I think I would rather hear about the don again.'

Catalina thought about the stories she had been re-reading lately with Lydia. Don Quixote and his endless quest for a perfect world that always eluded him. For a life that could never be. 'I cannot think of a story for right now.'

'Then will you sing that song for me again, Catalina? The one you once taught me when we walked together in Spain,' Jamie said softly. She felt the soft brush of his breath against her shoulder and realised he had moved even closer to her as they talked. She nodded, but she feared her voice would strangle in her throat at his nearness. She touched the tip of her tongue to her dry lips and slowly began to sing, wobbly and off-key.

'Conde Niño, por amores es niño y pasó a la mar; va a dar aqua a su...'

But she couldn't finish. Jamie's lips came down on hers, swallowing the song, her breath, her everything. She was surrounded only by him, by the heat and scent of him, the force of his passion that drew out her own desire all over again.

With a low moan, her arms came around him tightly as she rolled to her back, drawing him down with her, onto her. She had tried so hard to force away her feelings for him, to shatter them into oblivion, but they wouldn't leave. They burst free at his touch, like brilliant flashes of fireworks in a dark sky. She needed him now; her desire was a force as free and elemental as the storm outside.

Jamie couldn't be hers for ever, but he was hers right now. Just as she was, and always would be, his.

Catalina impatiently pushed the blanket away from his body. It draped to his hips, leaving his chest bare for her seeking caress. He was everything she had remembered in her dreams, his skin like hot, smooth satin over lean muscle and bone, shifting and bunching under her touch. She ran her fingernails lightly along the long line of his back, to the swell of his buttocks and then up again to twine in his hair and hold him with her.

He groaned as his tongue slid into her mouth, all a heated rush of breath and need. It wasn't a careful, seductive kiss, but one rough with long-denied passion. Catalina's hand threaded deeper into his hair, drawing him even closer, while her other hand slid over his shoulder to feel the pattern of those scars on her palm.

The blanket still wrapped around her seemed to

abrade her sensitised skin with its texture and she shoved it away. Jamie reached down to help her, stripping the coverings away until she lay bare beneath him. She raised her leg and used her foot to push his own blanket all the way off before she wrapped her thigh around his waist. At last they were skin to skin, their bodies together. His chest slid over her breasts, raising her nipples to hard, sensitive points. She moaned and wrapped her other leg around him so he could not escape her.

Wrapped in the unreality of the storm, they were free.

Her head fell back as his lips trailed a ribbon of hot kisses down her throat and over her bare shoulder. She arched up into him and felt the heavy heat of his erection against her hip. He wanted her too, as much as she wanted him.

'Jamie,' she whispered. *'Amado.'*

'Catalina,' he groaned. 'Catalina, how I have missed you.' His tongue traced lightly on the soft curve of her breast. His fingertips circled one of her nipples just before he rose up above her and closed his lips around it hard, drawing it deep into his mouth.

She sobbed out incoherent Spanish love words,

until slowly his mouth drew away and he breathed a light caress over her pebbled flesh.

'Open to me again, Catalina,' he whispered. She felt his hand against her thigh, moving softly closer and closer to where she longed for him to touch her damp core. 'Open to me.'

'Yes,' she answered, and her thighs parted at his coaxing caress. She couldn't breathe, couldn't move with the ache of her desire for him. His fingers delved ever so lightly along the opening of her womanhood, teasing her.

'Please!' she gasped, arching her back.

'Do you want more, Catalina?' he said roughly. 'Just as I do?' He knelt between her legs and slid one long finger deeply inside of her. His touch curled, seeking that one small spot that had always made her cry out. It still did, and she called his name as the fiery sensations shot through her.

'You're so wet,' Jamie muttered. 'And tight. Has it been a while?'

She nodded. 'Since—since the last time we were together.'

He went very still above her, as if her words surprised him. She feared he might draw away from her, ask her about the years they had been apart—but this was no time for words.

She reached out and ran her fingers lightly along the hot, taut satin of his erection. She felt the tracery of veins there and pressed her touch harder to the pulsing head, just as she remembered he liked. His breath drew in sharply and he seemed to grow even harder in her hand.

'Don't leave me,' she whispered. 'It's been too long.'

'Oh, Catalina,' he groaned. 'I could never leave you.' He kissed her again, deeply with the force of unstoppable need. It had been much too long.

Catalina welcomed his kiss joyfully and wrapped her legs around his waist as she felt the tip of his manhood slide against her. He thrust inside her, one exquisite movement at a time. She held on to his shoulders, his skin damp against her hands, and closed her eyes as she felt him joined with her again at last.

She opened her eyes and stared up into the grey heat of his gaze as he slowly moved within her. The pleasure of being with him again spread through her like the lightning outside, quick flashes of heat, delight that built and built until it was too great to contain. It thundered in her mind, and everything vanished but the feel of his skin against hers, the movement of his body inside hers. She heard his low moan and cried out in answer.

'Catalina!' he shouted as his body arched above hers. 'Catalina.'

'Jamie, *amado*.' She fell back into their nest of blankets, weak and still filled with the bright glow of pleasure. It was all even better than her memories and dreams.

Jamie collapsed beside her, his head on her shoulder, and she gently reached up to caress his damp hair. This moment was perfect, and Catalina knew that no matter what came after she would always have this.

Jamie slowly sank down into the blankets by her side. His arm came around her waist, holding her close as their breathing slowed and the air grew chilly around them again. Catalina could feel dark, exhausted oblivion encroaching on her, but she didn't want to slip away into sleep. Not yet. She wanted to hold on to this moment with Jamie as long as she could.

She rolled onto her side and studied him in

the light from the fading embers of the fire. He looked relaxed and sleepy, and so very young. The austere lines of his face were softened, burnished by the firelight. His hair was tousled, tumbling over his brow.

His hand rose lazily and caressed gently over her shoulder.

'We should go back to the house,' she whispered.

Jamie shook his head without opening his eyes. 'Not until the rain stops. We have time yet.'

Time before the real world closed in on them again—but not much. Already Catalina could feel its sands running out around her. She rested her head on his chest and closed her eyes to listen to the rhythm of his heartbeat.

'What happened in Spain, Jamie?' she asked quietly. 'After—after you thought I died.'

The hand that caressed her shoulder paused for a tiny second before its rhythm resumed, just as soft and careful as before.

After a long moment, he said, 'That is a tale that is quite dull, I fear. It should wait for another day.' He sat up, and Catalina watched as he knelt by the fire to stir up its dying embers. The long, lean line of his naked back gleamed in the light. Catalina drew the blankets up around her, and she knew he would tell her nothing today.

'But what happened then is why I cannot condemn Miss Walters, as my family would do,' he said quietly. 'She made a terrible mistake out of desperation, and she is paying for it now. She will pay for it in her soul for the rest of her life, knowing that she did such a thing.'

Catalina couldn't bear seeing the stark pain in his eyes. 'Jamie, whatever you did in Spain, whatever happened, it is past.'

'Is it?' Jamie shook his head. 'We carry our past with us wherever we go, Catalina. Surely you and I know that better than anyone. It's why I cannot condemn Alicia Walters.'

'But what she did to your family...'

'Was not entirely her own doing,' he said. 'Do you remember a man called Hugh Webster?'

Catalina shuddered at the mention of that name. It was a name she had not heard in so long, but she remembered him. The horrible panic she had felt when he grabbed her. 'Of course I remember him, the vile man.'

'It was he who concocted the scheme of setting up Alicia as my widow at Castonbury,' Jamie said. 'He who had taken my lost signet ring. She began because she was desperate to protect her child, but he forced her to continue. And now he has disappeared.'

'Webster?' Catalina cried, appalled. 'But what has happened to him? How could he have done such a thing and just vanished?'

'That is what I am trying to discover. And Alicia has agreed to help me. Once Webster has paid for his crimes, I will help her start over somewhere away from here.'

Start over. Somewhere with him? Did he truly care about Alicia? She had seen how they greeted each other at that house....

No. She shook her head. She had no right to be jealous any longer, no matter who he cared about or what he did. She had to put all that aside, to forget everything that had happened. At least for now. One day he would have to tell her what happened in Spain.

'I want to help you,' she said quietly. 'I know we can find Webster if we work together.'

'Catalina, no,' Jamie protested. 'The man is clearly mad. I won't put you in danger.'

'I would be in no danger, not with you,' Catalina argued. 'Webster did terrible things, both in Spain and here. I want to see him stopped, just as you do. I know I can help.'

'We can talk about all this later,' Jamie said, and Catalina recognised the stubborn set of his jaw. He would not argue with her, yet he would stand very firm.

But she was as stubborn as him. 'Yes, we will assuredly talk about it later,' she insisted.

A rueful smile touched his lips. 'It's late now, Catalina. You should rest a little longer. The rain will surely stop soon.'

Catalina nodded, suddenly realising that she was indeed very weary. So much had happened, her mind was spinning with it. 'Only for a little while. We must be back at Castonbury before it grows too late.'

'I will keep watch,' he said, and she knew he would keep his word. She lay back down on her side facing the fire and let its warmth and heat wrap around her.

As sleep closed in on her mind, she felt Jamie tuck the blankets over her and she smiled. For the first time in a very, very long while, she felt safe....

* * *

Catalina's slender body was relaxed and warm in the circle of his arms, her hair falling like a skein of dark satin across his chest. He ran his palm gently over her hair, along the curve of her back. She shivered against him in her sleep and he drew her closer.

They were as close as a man and woman could possibly be, their bodies wrapped around each other after the heated rush of sex, yet it seemed like she was still a thousand miles away from him. His Catalina—more elusive than ever. He had almost thought he was drawing her close to him again, that they were almost as they had been in Spain—able to read each other without even speaking. Then she had pulled away from him again.

Ever since he had first glimpsed Catalina across that camp in Spain, she had intrigued him, drawn him in with just one glance from her dark eyes. Talking with her had only made him want to know more and more, craved her presence, within the spell she wove with her smile and her touch.

And his memories of their lovemaking, memories he had treasured on so many lonely nights,

were as nothing compared to the reality of tonight. The reality of being with her, touching
her, feeling her against him. Never had he felt as
he had this afternoon, when his body had joined
with Catalina's, and he had opened his eyes to
see that she really was there beneath him, her
head arched back, her lips parted. That reality
was beyond pleasure, beyond merely satisfying
his body's cravings. Beyond just the two of them,
Jamie and Catalina, at that moment.

He had thought his heart would burst with the
joy, the triumph of holding her again.

Now, with the cold night closing around them
and her sleeping next to him, he could see that
she was still not his. She said she could not truly
be his wife. She pushed him away and he didn't
know why. His family wanted him to marry but
his Catalina had come back to him. No matter
what she said, he couldn't be free of her nor she
of him. They were married. The only thing that
made any practical sense was to acknowledge that
and learn to make a new life together.

Catalina murmured in her sleep and he closed
his arms around her. He had to make her see
sense, that was all. Yet he could tell she had lost

none of her Spanish stubborn spirit, that in fact it had grown over the years. She was determined to do what was right as she saw it, but then so was he.

He owed Catalina for all she had suffered in the years since they parted. He had to make it up to her somehow, to make sure she was cared for. He only needed a plan to make her see that, to make her let him help her. His proud Spanish lady.

Jamie tightened his arms around her and he breathed in the sweet scent of her hair. For just a moment he let himself feel the exultation of being here with Catalina again, his beautiful, lost Catalina, and forget everything else. Holding her there in his arms, he let himself find the first restful sleep he had known in years.

Catalina slowly drifted up from the haze of dreams. She couldn't remember what her visions were while she slept, but she somehow knew they were sweet because she felt peaceful and content as she hadn't in so very long. Smiling, she stretched out beneath the rough wool blanket— and then she felt a large, warm hand at her waist.

And she remembered *everything*. Jamie and

their lovemaking. How strong and sweet and perfect it had been, just like in her memories. She rolled onto her side and studied his face in the dying light of the fire.

His dark hair was rumpled over his forehead, and asleep he looked so much younger. The sharpness of his features was relaxed, his wariness and watchfulness gone for the moment. Catalina felt as if she was seeing him as he must have been long ago, before the horrors of Spain and the burdens of his family had descended on him.

Before he married her.

Filled with the longing to give him back that lost peace, that idyll, Catalina leaned towards him and softly pressed her lips to his. Jamie moaned as he woke up to her kiss, and she felt his hand gently caress her cheek, the loose fall of her hair. She drew back to look deeply into his eyes, those beautiful grey eyes, and let herself have this too-short, eternal moment with him.

'Catalina,' he whispered, and claimed her lips again in a fierce, desperate kiss.

She needed him so much, and in that kiss she could tell he needed her too. Through the blurry haze of desire, she felt his hands close around her hips and he shifted their bodies so that she lay on top of him. His tongue traced the curve of her lower lip, softly, teasingly, before he slid inside.

Catalina moaned at the taste of him, so familiar and yet so strange at the same time. His kiss trailed away from her lips, over her cheek and along the curve of her throat. Jamie touched the tip of his tongue to her bare shoulder and then blew on it lightly until she shivered. That wild, yearning feeling inside of her expanded until she thought she might burst with it all. *He* did that, only Jamie.

He traced the edge of his teeth gently along her shoulder, making her shiver again, before he pressed an open-mouthed kiss on the soft spot where her shoulder met her neck. He drew the blanket away from her body and his hand traced the edge of her waist and her abdomen, lower and lower, sliding aside the cloth until she was bare to him.

Catalina tilted back her head and stared up at his face, chiselled and half shadowed in the firelight. His grey eyes glittered in the darkness, and his lips curved in a smile that made her smile too.

This was her Jamie, the man she had married. The man she had missed.

She traced a light touch slowly up his chest and felt the strong, hard heat of him. He was so very alive under her caress, so wondrous. And he made her feel as if she was coming back to life too, after she had felt so cold and numb for so long. And she was intoxicated with that feeling, with being with him again at last.

She felt his stomach muscles tighten as her hand slid lower and lower. The tips of her fingers brushed his erection and she felt him harden even more.

'Catalina…' he said tightly, but he didn't move under her touch. He just watched her closely with those jewel-like eyes.

Catalina smiled, and slid her palms up over his chest and touched every inch of him. Full of wonder, she traced a soft caress over his strong shoulders, down his corded arms, her fingertips fluttering over his chest. He seemed thinner than he had been in Spain, leaner, harder, but she was still fascinated by every inch of him, by being close to him.

Yet even as she let herself fall deep into that

swirling pool of desire for him, she knew how dangerous it could all be. She couldn't afford to forget how much lay between them now, a gulf of years and memories. But for this one moment, surrounded by the rain and the firelight, she could forget—with Jamie.

She closed her eyes and arched closer to him. Every breath she took, full of the scent of him, seemed to draw him to her even more. She pressed her parted lips to his bare chest, and tasted the warm, damp salt of his skin. She could feel his heartbeat against her, fast and frantic, echoing her own. She let the tip of her tongue swirl around his flat nipple.

Jamie let her explore, let her feel her freedom. She curled her arms around him and traced her touch down his spine to pull him closer to her. Her hands moved down, down, slowly, teasingly, until her fingers curled over his hard buttocks.

And then his control shattered. 'Catalina,' he groaned, and his hands closed around her waist. Catalina laughed and wrapped her legs around his hips. He kissed her, so hard and hot, so full of raw, burning need. She arched her hips up tight into his and the blurry haze of sexual need closed around them, and she held on to him as she fell down into it.

What was it about *this* man that made her feel that way? She didn't know, and at the moment she didn't care.

'Catalina.' His mouth slid from hers to kiss her jaw, her shoulder, to linger on that sensitive spot on her neck. When she sighed and let her head fall back to the blankets, he reached up to touch her soft, aching nipple.

'Catalina, you are so beautiful,' he whispered. He traced the tip of his tongue along the soft underside of her breast, teasing her.

Catalina reached up to tangle her fingers in the rough silk of his hair and held him against her. Finally, as she murmured wordless entreaties, he gave her what she longed for and took her nipple deep into his mouth. As his tongue swirled around it, his fingers caressed her other breast, gently, expertly. He rolled and stroked the nipple until she cried out his name.

His mouth traced a ribbon of kisses on the soft skin between her breasts, and Catalina reached out blindly between their bodies to unfasten the front of his trousers. He sprang into her hand, hard, hot, the veins throbbing under her touch, and she felt a surge of triumph that he wanted her as much as she wanted him. In this, as always, they were together.

She ran a slow, caressing touch up the full length of him, then pressed closer as he moaned. His finger lightly traced her womanhood before sliding deep inside of her. The rough friction of his touch against the soft wetness made her cry out. Her back arched up from the blankets and her eyes closed as the feelings washed over her.

His thumb rubbed hard against that tiny, hidden spot up high inside her, and it felt as if white-hot sparks raced through her.

'Catalina,' he whispered against her neck as he kissed her there again and again. 'Tell me you want me. Tell me you missed me as I missed you.'

For an instant she thought there was a strange, yearning note in his deep voice, but when she opened her eyes to look up at him his face was drawn taut into inscrutable, unreadable lines.

'I want you,' she said simply.

Jamie nodded, and his hand slid down to press her legs open to him. And with a twist of his hips, he thrust deeply into her.

Catalina gasped at the sensation of being joined with him again. Her legs closed tighter around him and she fell down and down into the pleasure. She held on to him as he drew back and lunged forward again and again, deeper, harder. The scent and burning heat of him surrounded her and she moved with him, seeking her own pleasure. Their bodies and their breath were like one in that single perfect moment.

The sparkling, tingling pressure built and built deep inside of her, growing and expanding like the night sky until it exploded.

'Jamie, *mi corazón*!' she cried, holding on to him as if he was the only thing left in a drowning world.

He threw his head back, his whole body taut above her as he came. 'Catalina,' he shouted, and then slowly collapsed beside her on the blankets, his shoulders shaking. His breath seemed harsh in the sudden silence, and Catalina feared she couldn't catch her own. She closed her eyes to try to hold on to that moment as long as she could.

'Catalina,' he whispered, and she felt him move to rest his head on her midriff, just below her bare breasts. His hair brushed softly against her skin, and she reached down to thread her fingers through it.

A strange kind of peace flowed through Catalina as she lay there wrapped in Jamie's arms, and at first she didn't know what that feeling was. She hadn't known such an instant of warmth and perfect contentment in a long time, as if that was exactly where she was meant to be. She felt Jamie press a soft kiss against her skin and she smiled.

Soon, much too soon, this rainy afternoon would be over and she would have to face the truth of the past and of their situation now. But right now she was with him as she had never thought to be again, and it was precious.

Chapter Fourteen

'Do stand still for a moment, Lydia, or your hem will be uneven,' Catalina said, but she couldn't help but laugh. Lydia's enthusiasm was infectious, and she made even the greyish day outside seem brighter.

As did memories of two nights ago, when she had slept for a time in Jamie's arms. She knew it had been a mistake, that she should forget about it now, but still she smiled at the wondrous feelings that lingered. The magic between her and Jamie was still there, no matter what. That gave her something to secretly remember and cherish.

'I am trying to be still, Mrs Moreno, truly,' Lydia said as Catalina put the final stitches in the hem of her costume. 'I am just very excited about the play tonight! What if I forget my lines?'

'You won't. Haven't you been practising all day?'

'I just want it all to be perfect.' Lydia bit her lip. 'Do you think Mr Hale will be there?'

Catalina heard the note of hope and fear in Lydia's voice, the note that said *this* was really what she had been fidgeting about. Seeing the handsome curate again. She sat back on her heels and looked up at Lydia. The girl's cheeks turned pink and she looked away to fuss with her costume skirt.

Oh, dear, Catalina thought. Her charge was infatuated with Mr Hale. He seemed a very respectable young man, and she had seen at the Assembly Rooms that he admired Lydia as well. But Lydia's guardian seemed to have his own hopes that she would marry the duke. It had always been an unlikely prospect with Jamie, but the step down from a duke to a curate didn't seem like one her family would likely countenance.

And Catalina couldn't bear to see the sweet girl hurt.

'There will be many people there, I'm sure,' Catalina said carefully. 'They are all sure to admire your performance. But don't forget the wedding will be over in a few days and we'll be going back to London.'

And she would not see Jamie again. A spasm of pain rippled over Catalina at the thought, but she pushed it away to keep her smile cool and unwavering. She stood up and busied herself gathering up the thread and pins.

'Oh, yes,' Lydia said quietly. 'I had almost forgot we will have to leave.'

'You are enjoying yourself here at Castonbury?'

'So very much! I was silly to be so nervous about coming here. I love the country so much more than Town. Everyone is so kind, no one stares or laughs.…'

Catalina glanced over to see that Lydia was staring out of the window. A stage was being erected in the gardens for that evening's theatricals and garden party, and Mr Hale had just joined the men who were working on its construction. The handsome young man was laughing, and Lydia looked so full of wistful longing as she watched him.

'Lydia, my dear,' Catalina said. She gently took the girl's arm and turned her away from the window. 'Life in London is not so grey as all that, you know. You have much to look forward to there.'

'Do I?'

'Of course. There will be dances and concerts, the theatre—and you are sure to find a suitor to your liking there. One your guardian will also like.'

Lydia nodded, but Catalina could see that she was not convinced. And why should she be? Mr Hale was a very respectable choice, especially for a young lady of Lydia's disposition. Young lovers shouldn't be parted because of ambition or duty. Catalina knew the pain that caused all too well. She had to help Lydia be cautious, but not to lose hope too soon.

'Let's go over your lines again,' Catalina said, taking up the script from the table.

An hour later, there was a knock at the door. Catalina opened it to find a footman standing there with a note in his hand. His blond hair contrasted with the red and gold of his livery, and his eyes were strangely insolent as he looked at her. 'Excuse me, Mrs Moreno, but I was asked to deliver this to you,' he said.

'Thank you.' Catalina took the note, and saw

that it was Jamie's handwriting that spelled her name across the folded paper. Breathless, she hastily closed the door and broke the wax seal to open it.

Catalina. I have not been able to see you alone for the past few days, and I fear we may not have the chance to speak privately again for a while. But I must tell you so many things—beginning with what happened to me in Spain after I thought you died...
I cared for nothing at all when you were gone. I felt cold, removed, and it didn't matter what happened or what I did. I infiltrated a group opposed to the king in order to send their plans to the British government. I came to believe what I did was painful but necessary for the security of Europe after Napoleon, and as I did not care if I lived or died it seemed best I was the one to do this rather than a man with a wife. When I was discovered, there was a fight and I was wounded, as you can see now.
It was soon after that my brother Harry found me and I heard what had really happened at

Castonbury while I was gone—the financial troubles, the scandal, father's health. I had abandoned them when they needed me the most, and only then did I feel the full weight of my mistakes. I can only try and make it right now, for all of us.

And that is why I truly cannot bring myself to hate Alicia Walters. I have done things as terrible as she has, and yet here I have another chance with my family.

If you can, please meet me tomorrow. I will send you word on where and when. I must see you and talk to you more. J.

Catalina closed her eyes and clutched the note tightly in her hand. How Jamie must have hurt, so ill, so far from home! And she had not been there to comfort him. She still could not, not really. She feared he wouldn't accept any comfort she could give anyway. So much had happened while they were parted, so much that she didn't know. If they were to be together again, they would have to find a way past that, and she wasn't sure that was even possible any longer.

Yet still there was that temptation to meet him,

to run to him. She urged prudence on Lydia, but it seemed she had none herself. She never had, not when it came to Jamie.

Catalina went to the window and looked down at the small garden below. It was much quieter there than in the grand front gardens. No one rushed around getting ready for the party tonight. But the peaceful scene brought no quiet to her own heart.

'Oh, Jamie,' she whispered. 'Why do you do this to me?'

Why did he make it so very hard to do what she knew she had to do?

'...though you have ever had my heart, yet now I find I love you more because I bring you less!'

As Lydia swooned back in the leading man's arms for the final time, everyone applauded and cheered enthusiastically.

Catalina couldn't help but smile at Lydia's glowing face as the girl took her bow. The Chinese lanterns strung around the stage added an otherworldly glow to the late evening. The grey skies had miraculously lifted before the play began and now the sunset was bright pink with gold streaks along the edge of the horizon. More lights were strung in the trees, and the guests were seated in rows of white and gold chairs on the grass. Everyone from the family and local gentry to the estate tenants and villagers were dressed in their finest and everyone was laughing and having a fine time.

It made Catalina's heart feel lighter to see it. Castonbury was its own small world, and a happier one now that Jamie was home and there was a wedding to look forward to. It was a perfect warm summer evening, a moment of brightness after the gloom of years.

Catalina glanced over her shoulder to where Jamie sat with his father on the back row of chairs. The duke's armchair had been brought out for him, and after much complaining and threatening to leave early, he had been wrapped in shawls and persuaded to stay. Even he looked happy as he clapped for the play, and leaned over to say something to Jamie.

Jamie shook his head and gave that crooked half-smile of his. As he said something in reply to his father, he caught her looking at him and actually gave her a wink.

Catalina spun back around to face the stage and tried not to laugh. It was a strange night indeed.

The actors took their last bows and yielded the stage to the musicians who were to play for the evening's dancing. As they tuned up, footmen hurried out to take up the chairs and everyone lined up along the refreshment tables. Lily and Giles themselves were handing out glasses of punch and accepting best wishes.

Catalina had been told such a gathering was a tradition at Castonbury, a time for everyone around the estate to gather and celebrate a marriage. But it had not been held in many years, not since the duke had married his late duchess.

'It will be a joyous day indeed when Lord Hatherton and his bride have their own party,' Mrs Stratton had said. 'Castonbury will be truly back to itself then.'

Lord Hatherton. It had been so easy to forget who Jamie was when he held her in his arms in that rough little cottage as the rain fell around them. But here, with all the weight and tradition of Castonbury around them, with all the people who expected so much of their heir, she was reminded.

She found a quiet place to stand under a tree at the edge of the gathering where she could watch everyone. Couples were finding their way to the dance; Lydia was sipping punch with Mr Hale, giggling and blushing at something he said to her. Catalina hated to take her away from him just yet, not on such a night. The girl couldn't get into much trouble with the crowds around her.

Catalina drifted around the party, letting the lively music wash over her. The dancers were spinning and twirling, laughing with the sheer joy of the exercise, of dancing under the rising moon of a fine summer's night.

The garden folly, so silent and solitary as it watched over the gathering, glowed a pure white in the night. Catalina leaned her head against the trunk of a tree and looked at it, letting the memory of her kiss there with Jamie wash over her. That was what she was doing here—building up a store of memories to carry forward with her. She could take them out like beautiful tiny jewels on cold nights to come and they would sustain her.

Suddenly the serene scene was broken by a figure running across the meadow. It was a tall man clad in dark clothes, and surely could be anyone at the party. But something about the way he moved, so quick and furtive, made her frown as she watched him. Who would flee from the festivities like that?

Just before he reached the folly, his hat tumbled from his head. He paused for a moment to retrieve it, and as he bent down the moonlight caught on his bright-coloured hair. Then he was gone.

Catalina started to run after him, but one step reminded her she only wore thin evening slippers. She could never catch him, and even if she did what would she say? Lecture him about leaving parties early?

She shook her head. It was only Jamie telling her that it was Hugh Webster behind Alicia's scheme, and the bad memories that awoke, making her think she saw him. Hugh Webster.

Yet there had been that man she saw at the Assembly Rooms as well...

'Mrs Moreno?' she heard Lydia say. She turned to see the girl walking towards her, the Chinese lanterns bright on her filmy white costume. 'Are you all right?'

Catalina smiled. 'Very well. I was just getting

a breath of air. You were splendid in the play, Lydia.'

'Oh, Mrs Moreno, I had so much fun!' Lydia cried happily. 'I wish there could be a party like this every night.'

'You would soon tire of it if there was.'

'I never could.' Lydia's smile suddenly faded and she bit her lip uncertainly. 'But did you see that strange man?'

A bolt of alarm shot through Catalina. 'Strange man?'

'Yes, it was the oddest thing. He wasn't dressed up for the party or anything. He was just standing there alone, just beyond the stage.' Lydia gestured towards the corner of the stage where the musicians now played. It was half hidden by a drapery. 'He seemed to be watching Lord Hatherton, and he looked almost…angry.'

'You didn't speak to him, did you?' Catalina said urgently.

'Certainly not. He looked too fearsome, so glowering. I pointed him out to Mr Hale, but by then he was gone.'

'Could you tell what he looked like?'

'Not really. It was too dark there. But he was

rather tall, and had an unusual red beard.' Lydia's eyes widened. 'Who do you think he is, Mrs Moreno? A criminal escaped from gaol or something like that?'

Catalina tried to laugh to reassure Lydia. It would never do to frighten the girl, yet it did sound rather like Hugh Webster. He surely wasn't as safely far away as Jamie seemed to think. 'No, of course not. Probably just an uninvited guest. But if you do see someone like that again, be sure and let me know at once.'

'Of course, Mrs Moreno.'

Catalina led Lydia back to the bright lights of the party, and soon the girl was dancing with Phaedra's handsome husband, Bram. Once she was sure Lydia was safely occupied, she went in search of Jamie.

Fortunately she found him alone, watching the dancers. He gave her a smile as she joined him. 'Having a good time?' he said.

'Yes, quite,' Catalina answered in a soft voice. 'Your family does know how to give a good party. Yet I fear there was an interloper here earlier.'

Jamie's expression didn't change, but she saw his jaw tighten. 'An interloper?'

'Yes. I saw him run off through the gardens, and Lydia glimpsed him over by the stage. She said he had a red beard. Could it be Webster?'

'Neither of you approached him, did you?' Jamie asked sharply.

'No, not at all. I didn't even see him very clearly.'

'Good. Stay right here for a moment, Catalina.'

He turned away and she caught his arm. 'You can't go chasing after him! He is probably long gone by now. And...' And she couldn't bear to see him hurt again.

'I won't be gone long.'

Then he left her there. Catalina waited anxiously, watching the party, wondering what Jamie was doing, where he had gone. She scanned each face, making sure none of them were Webster. After what felt like hours, but was probably only about fifteen minutes, he reappeared at her side.

'I have sent some of the footmen to search the grounds,' he said, 'but I am sure you are right. If it is Webster, he is long gone. If it wasn't for the party he could never have got on Castonbury property. I should have been more vigilant.'

'Not in such a crowd as this,' Catalina protested. 'But why would he be here instead of flee-ing abroad somewhere? Surely he knows he has been discovered.'

Jamie shrugged, but she could see his tension in the set of his shoulders, the sharp watchfulness in his eyes as he scanned the dancers. 'I will find out soon enough. He can't hide for ever.'

Catalina was sure he could not, not from Jamie. But Webster had to be underhanded and unscru-pulous to come up with such a scheme, and she didn't want to see Jamie hurt again. 'You will be careful?'

He smiled down at her. 'I am always careful, Catalina.'

She doubtfully studied the scar on his cheek. 'I want to help you.'

'I won't put you in danger,' he said.

'I won't be,' Catalina protested. 'But I can be good at watching and observing. Perhaps I can hear some gossip about the man, ask around to see if anyone glimpsed him without knowing it.'

Jamie was quiet for a long moment, and Catalina thought he would refuse to let her help at all. But then he nodded shortly. 'Tomorrow Lily is taking some of the guests on a picnic to gather wild strawberries. Lydia can go with them, if you would care to accompany me to Alicia's house and talk this over with her. She thought she saw Webster a few nights ago as well.'

Jamie wanted her to see Alicia with him? Catalina looked away, not sure what to say. She hadn't really seen Alicia since Spain, only that quick glimpse when Jamie had met her at the house in Buxton. She had no idea what she could say to her. Yet she had the strongest feeling that Hugh Webster had to be caught, no matter what it took.

'Was he not her conspirator?' she said. 'Are you certain she has not been in contact with him?'

'Quite sure. She proved herself to be an adequate actress with my family, but she is not that good. I could see the true fear in her eyes when she spoke of Webster. He had her, and all my family, in his power for too long. He surely won't walk away from all that without a fight.'

Catalina turned his words over in her mind. Bullies like Webster might hide like the cowards they were when directly confronted, but they would wait and scheme to get what they wanted. She had met too many people just like that in her life. Webster had thought he had a grand prize in his sights; he would be enraged at losing it and would surely blame Jamie for that. Webster had hated him so much even in Spain.

She looked back at the party. Everyone was laughing and dancing, having a splendid time, and Castonbury stood as the glowing, glittering backdrop. A symbol of permanence and tradition that she had come to feel such fondness for. A man like Webster couldn't be allowed to mar even a stone of it. Not if she could help it at all.

'I will go with you to see Alicia, then,' Catalina said. 'But now I have to return to Lydia.'

'We still have things to talk about, Catalina,' he said.

She nodded. She knew he was right. 'I will meet you later, then.'

And she walked back towards the gathering to find Lydia. Soon enough she would have to leave Jamie and Castonbury, just as she had warned Lydia. At least this way she could help to make sure that, after all their troubles, they were safe again.

Catalina paced the length of the folly, her footsteps echoing on the stone floor. It was the only sound she could hear in the quiet, silent darkness of the night. Even the birds were quiet in the trees.

Beyond the marble pillars, over the black-green of the lawns, the house was quiet too. A few lights glowed in the windows here and there, tiny beacons in the night, but most of the inhabitants of the house were safely asleep.

As Catalina should be, she knew that. But she couldn't sleep yet. She had to talk to Jamie again, alone, before she could think about what to do next. Before she could see Alicia Walters and know what steps she should take.

She looked down at Jamie's letter, held tightly in her hand. So many thoughts and emotions had gone through her when she had read those words, as if the chaos of the past and the confusion of the present had collided and mixed into one inextricable blur. She had thought when she came to England she could leave Spain and all that happened there behind, but it was always with her.

The one thing she could see clearly, though, was that her feelings for Jamie had not changed. That overwhelming connection she had sensed the very first time she saw him had only strengthened and deepened, and she couldn't quite imagine going away from Castonbury and never seeing him again. A part of her would always be here with him.

She looked down again at the letter. After all that had happened, could they be together? Was there any way at all? Or would the past always haunt them?

Catalina laughed at herself. She didn't even really know what Jamie thought of her now, what he wanted from her. Now that he was at home with his family, perhaps he felt the folly of war-time romance. Perhaps this letter was only his final apology, his goodbye.

Suddenly a noise out in the garden interrupted her thoughts. For an instant she remembered the man she had glimpsed running through the garden at the party and her hand tightened on the letter, crumpling it.

Then she saw the tall, lean figure moving through the moonlight and relief rushed through her. *Jamie*—of course. She was meant to be meeting him here, after all.

'Catalina,' he said as he climbed the steps to the folly. He stopped by her side, not touching her but close. 'You came.'

'Of course,' she said. She couldn't stay away from him, even when she knew she should. She saw him glance at the letter in her hand.

'You received it, then,' he said.

'Yes,' Catalina answered quietly. She slowly reached out with her free hand and gently brushed her fingertips over his cheek, the scars there. He grew tense, yet he didn't draw away. He swayed closer, as if against his will, and suddenly she ached for all he had suffered. All they had *both* suffered. 'I am sorry you were hurt.'

Jamie shook his head. 'I deserved it. I never should have been there in the first place, as you tried to tell me. I thought I was protecting my family, my country. But in the end that belief was false, an illusion. Like so much else.'

Like their marriage? Had that been an illusion too? Sometimes Catalina was sure it must have been; real life was harsh and cold, never that beautiful. But then sometimes, when he stood close to her as he was now, she thought it had been the most real thing ever.

'War is a terrible thing,' she said. 'It takes everything we believe about ourselves and strips it all away. It's hard to tell what is real and necessary and what isn't. You did what you felt you must do, and you paid a price for it that no one should have to.'

'But you have paid that price as well, Catalina,' he said roughly. 'And that is the damnable thing. That is what I can't forgive myself for. When I thought you were dead, that I could never explain or make it up to you...' His words broke off as he shook his head.

Catalina's heart ached as if it would break all over again. She moved closer to Jamie and reached up to take his beautiful, damaged face in her hands. 'I am alive! We are both alive, and we can hear each other now. That's the important thing, Jamie, *mi corazón*. Tell me whatever you want now, and I will hear and understand.'

Rather than talk though, Jamie curled his hands around her bare arms and pressed her back against the cool marble column. He held her there gently, but Catalina knew she couldn't break away from him. His body was so close to hers, she could feel every inch of his warm hardness against her, and she wanted to press even closer. To curl herself up in him and never be apart from him again.

It was the most bittersweet longing. She tilted

back her head to stare at the stark lines of his austere face in the chalk-white light, as if she could memorise him.

'Catalina, Catalina,' he said, and she could hear an echoing longing in his voice. 'I only ever wanted to make you smile, to make you happy, but instead I ruined everything. Yet I can't stay away from you. Why do you make me so insane?'

Catalina shook her head, her thoughts spinning madly. *He* made her insane. He took her out of herself until she no longer knew what to do.

'Jamie, I...' she whispered. She stared up into his eyes, until with a groan his head swooped down over hers. His lips met the soft curve of her neck, and her knees grew weak at the touch of his kiss. His arms tightened around her, holding her up as she fell.

'Jamie,' she gasped, and his mouth came hard over hers to catch the sound.

His tongue slid over hers and she met him, passion for passion. She twined her arms around his neck and wound her fingers through his hair. He lifted her high against the column and she wrapped her legs around his waist as her skirts fell around them to bind them together.

It took only that, a touch, a kiss, a look, to ignite the fire between them. She wanted it, wanted *him* so much, and yet it frightened her too.

Jamie seemed to sense her confusion, for his kiss trailed from her mouth and he rested his head on her shoulder as he held her there. They were so, so close, but also so far.

'Forgive me, Catalina,' he said. 'That is what I've wanted to say for all these years. Forgive me.'

'I do forgive you,' she answered. 'You did what you felt you had to.'

'Forgive—but not forget?'

She had no answer for that. She could only hold on to him for that moment and hope that was enough.

Chapter Fifteen

It was a lovely day, Catalina thought as she leaned back on the fine leather seats of Jamie's curricle. The sun was shining in a pale blue sky and the breeze smelled of flowers and fresh earth. She had seen Lydia off on her picnic excursion and then walked out of the Castonbury gates and across the Park to meet Jamie, which gave her a chance to look at the land in all its glory. All its beautiful potential to be as grand as it once was.

It was a day she wished would never quite end. The sun on her face, Jamie by her side—it was perfect. And so was the forgiveness they had exchanged; the past was in the past. It had to be.

'What are you smiling about, Catalina?' Jamie asked. She glanced at him from under the brim of her bonnet to see that he smiled too.

The sight of it made her heart feel even lighter. He had always been such a serious man, ever since she first met him, but here at Castonbury he seemed to brood even more, as if so much hung over him. Yet his smile was so very beautiful. She wished she could see it every day.

'I was just thinking what a fine day it is,' she answered. 'Castonbury is such a lovely place.'

Jamie glanced at the fields to either side of the lane, endless expanses of green that rolled away to the horizon. The chimneys of the house could just be seen in the distance, like sentinels over this perfect little world.

'Yes,' he said quietly. 'It is a pretty place.'

'You must be glad to be home.'

Jamie was quiet for a long moment. 'I fear I had begun to forget what Castonbury looked like during my time in Spain. The details of it grew hazy in my mind, and I only remembered it as a sort of prison. A trap.'

'A trap?' Catalina said in surprise. 'Your home?'

'When I was younger, it never felt quite like my home. I grew up on tales of the great Montagues, of our ancestors who held this important place in

English history and accomplished so much to the glory of our name. I knew the stories were meant to make me feel my place in this line of greatness, but it always seemed so remote from what I felt inside. Castonbury felt like a chain to bind me.'

'And that was really why you went to Spain?' Catalina said quietly, afraid to shatter this moment of intimacy between them. Of truth. Of what they had built last night in the folly.

Jamie nodded. 'I had a wildness in me that had to find some way to escape. The army, fighting the enemy, it seemed like a way to do that.'

'To find your own place in the world.'

'Yes.' He glanced at her and she saw the dark shadow in his grey eyes. The same shadow that had seemed to hang over her own life for so long. 'I thought I could prove my own worth to myself there, away from my family.'

'When I was growing up I also learned so many tales of what was expected of me, as a Spanish woman, as a Perez promised to marry a Moreno. Every moment of my life was regimented. I was told how to do everything. And I could see the years stretching before me, more of the same,'

Catalina said. 'It made me want to scream, to beat my fists against it all until it let me free!'

'Yes,' Jamie said intensely. 'That was how I felt when I was younger. I was sure Giles or Harry would make a much better heir than me. They never seemed to have this—this darkness inside of them.'

Catalina smiled at him. 'I am sure they did not want the weight of those expectations any more than you did.'

Jamie laughed. 'No, indeed. Giles says he never had a happier day than when he learned I was returning and he would not have to be the duke. He and Lily can make their own life for themselves.'

Catalina wondered what that would be like, to make her own choices. She had tried it when she left Seville to nurse, and it had just led her here. 'My brother was also a man with all his family's hopes pinned on him. My mother wept for days when he ran away to work with the liberal factions against the king.'

'He was doing what he believed in, just as you did when you came to help our armies,' Jamie said. 'You were both very brave, credits to your family name.'

'Were we? My parents would never have thought so,' Catalina said quietly. 'My brother saw his hopes for Spain crushed, and I was selfish when I left my home in Seville. But I have no regrets, and neither would my brother. Our souls would have withered if we had stayed.' She laid her gloved hand gently over Jamie's where he held the reins. 'You have another chance here with your family, a chance to rebuild Castonbury as you think it should be. I could never have done that with my home. I could never have really belonged there.'

Jamie turned his hand to wrap his fingers around hers. 'Do you not think you could ever make Castonbury your home as well?'

'Castonbury?' Catalina cried, shocked. 'How could it be?'

'Do you not like it?'

'I...' She turned her head to look out at those distant chimneys again. She *could* like Castonbury, probably far too much. She also cared for Jamie far too much to be one of those chains he spoke of. 'I don't see how anyone could not like it. It's such a beautiful house.'

He shot her a crooked, rueful smile. 'Then it's merely the house's heir you don't like.'

'Oh, Jamie,' Catalina said with a laugh. 'I think you know that *dislike* is the furthest thing I feel for you.'

'Yet you will not do the sensible thing and be my wife again.'

Did he want her as his wife? It sounded suspiciously to her as if he wanted the matchmakers off his back, and being married to her would be a convenient way to do that. But eventually he would be sorry for that. 'It would not be so very sensible to put your family to yet another shock, so soon after you returned from the dead. I don't want to be another chain for you, Jamie.'

Jamie shook his head. 'I am not that wild boy any longer, Catalina. I learned my lesson very well in Spain. This is my place—this is my task in life.' He shot her a burning glance. 'I don't want to do it alone.'

'All the better to think this over very carefully,' Catalina said calmly, even as her heart ached. She wanted so much to be the one to help him, to stand with him. She truly still loved him, even more than she had in Spain. But she wanted him to love her too, not see her as a 'sensible' solution to his problem, one he would later regret.

The carriage rolled into town, and Catalina opened her parasol to shield her face from the sun and the glances of any passers-by. The streets were not crowded at that time of day, and they were soon drawing up at Alicia's house on its quiet street.

Jamie climbed down from the high seat and came around to help Catalina, his hand lingering on hers. She waited as he tied up the horse, surreptitiously studying the empty pavement from under her parasol.

'Do you think Webster could be watching us now?' she whispered.

'I hope so, the bastard,' Jamie said firmly. 'Alicia wrote to him that she was working on a new scheme concerning me and begged him to call on her and offer his assistance. She has not yet had a reply. He is probably hiding and watching, like the coward he is. Skulking around parties and assemblies.'

Catalina glanced up at the house, so serene behind its brick walls and shuttered windows. She hated the thought of a man like Webster watching it, plotting harm to the people inside. Even if it was Alicia Walters.

'What of her child?' Catalina asked as Jamie led her up the front steps and knocked at the door. 'Is he safe here?'

'I believe she has taken to leaving him with the neighbour, a kindly widow, at times,' he said. 'And I have been keeping watch.'

The door swung open and Alicia stood there. She looked older than Catalina remembered from Spain, her blue eyes red-rimmed and strained. Yet she still wore quiet, respectable clothes, her hair pinned back in a simple knot. Her eyes widened when she saw Catalina and she gave a quick curtsey.

'Mrs Moreno,' Alicia said. 'I am so glad you came.' She stepped aside to let them in. 'I was afraid you might not, and I did so want to talk to you.'

'It has been a long time since we last saw each other,' Catalina answered.

'Indeed. And so much has happened.' Alicia led them into a small sitting room where a tea tray waited. Children's toys were stacked neatly by the wall, and a work box sat open on a table. 'When

I learned you were alive, well—I was very glad to know it. You were very kind to me in Spain. You and Lord Hatherton both.'

And yet she had repaid him with deceptions. Catalina did not say it aloud, but Alicia blushed as if she guessed her thoughts.

Catalina suddenly felt terrible for judging her so hastily. Was she herself not deceiving Jamie's family? Had she not felt desperation and grief too? She sat down and accepted a cup of tea from Alicia.

'We have both had many trials in the past years,' Catalina said softly.

'But I fear mine have been of my own making,' Alicia answered.

'Have you heard from Webster?' Jamie asked.

Alicia shook her head. 'But I did think I saw him again last night, across the street. He does not trust me, I think, yet he is greedy enough to want a part in any new scheme. I am sure he will be quite desperate by now and will soon make his move.'

'We will be ready for him,' Jamie said. 'Mr Everett still asks about you, Miss Walters. He wants to help in any way he can.'

Mr Everett? The Castonbury estate manager? Catalina watched, intrigued, as Alicia's blush deepened.

'No, I won't have him in any trouble because of me,' Alicia said. 'But I am anxious to hear any other plan you might have, Lord Hatherton.'

They talked a little longer about possible ways to track down Webster, with Alicia casting shy glances Catalina's way, before the shadows of the day grew darker and Catalina and Jamie had to turn back towards Castonbury. They drove down the road for a while in silence, turning over everything they had heard from Alicia, until Jamie drew in the horse.

'Let us walk for a while,' he said. 'It's such a fine day.'

'What a good idea,' Catalina answered. It *was* a fine day, one of those rare perfect summer days that felt like they would last for ever but were then gone in an instant. Just like her time with Jamie.

He led the horse as they strolled down the lane, past the fields where men were working in the distance. Catalina took off her bonnet and let the sun wash over her.

'Does all this belong to Castonbury?' she asked, gesturing to the fields and the woods beyond.

'Yes,' Jamie said. 'And more just past that way that has been fallow for a long time. I have been consulting with many of the other farmers in the neighbourhood to see what best use they can be put to. There has been too much waste at Castonbury.'

'So you are turning farmer?' Catalina said with a teasing smile. 'I could not have envisioned it.'

Jamie laughed. 'I would not have thought it myself in my soldiering days. But I must do my best for Castonbury. Phaedra and her husband have made a good beginning with the stables here now. I can do my part with the farm and the tenants.'

'You were a formidable leader in Spain, Jamie,' she said. 'Your home will surely prosper with you here now.'

'Even if I know nothing about sheep or cows or crop rotations?'

'You will learn,' she said.

'I am trying. Once Webster is out of the way...'

'Which he will be very soon!'

'Then I can really turn my attention to the estate. But the house needs a mistress. It has not really had one since my mother died.'

A proper mistress for Castonbury—a proper duchess. Yes, that would be the crown of Jamie's homecoming, Catalina was sure of it. She looked out over the fields and imagined it as hers, as *theirs*. It would be a dream to build such a life here.

But she loved Jamie, and she couldn't be selfish, grasping on to what she wanted with no thought to what would be best for him. She would not let the past they shared tie him down now.

She smiled up at him. 'We should be getting back. They'll be returning from the picnic soon, and Lydia will be rushing to tell me all about it.'

Jamie raised his brow, and Catalina could tell he saw through her quick change of subject. But he let the topic of a duchess for Castonbury drop. 'Your charge is a charming young lady. You seem very fond of her.'

'I am. It has been a pleasure to spend time with her.'

'She appears to have an admirer in Mr Hale.'

'Yes. I am not sure I should encourage their attachment,' Catalina said.

'My sister says Mr Hale is considered quite eligible in the neighbourhood. All the young ladies wear their finest bonnets to Sunday services now, I hear.'

Catalina laughed. 'Her guardian did hope for a, shall we say, grander match. But I think a country vicarage would suit Miss Westman very well.'

'What if I were to put in a good word for Mr Hale with her guardian?'

When Jamie himself was meant to be the 'grander match'? Catalina wasn't sure it would help, but any ally she could find for Lydia would be welcome. 'That would be very kind of you, Jamie. Thank you.'

'I want to help you in any way I can, Catalina,' he said quietly. 'If you will only let me.'

Catalina wasn't sure what to say. Her heart was pounding at his words. She nodded silently, and they continued on with their walk in silence through the lovely summer day.

Jamie studied the way the sun shone on Catalina's hair, turning it to a gleaming ebony. She turned her face up to its warmth and smiled, and for a moment she looked so very happy.

He suddenly had the urgent desire to make her feel like that every day. To make all her moments happy and free of any care or trouble. Because all of the happiest moments in *his* life had been spent with her.

When he thought she was dead, everything had gone grey and blank. It had been one of the reasons he took on the secret task in Spain; without her he hadn't cared about anything. Perhaps he had even hoped he might truly die. But then he saw her again, here at Castonbury, and all seemed right again.

As he watched her smile up at the sun, it hit him like an explosion—Catalina was his wife. She had been since that day in Spain, and she always would be even if she pushed him away. He didn't know what her real reasons were for running from him now, but he would find them out and overcome them all. He would find a way to make her stay.

Because he suddenly realised he could not go on without her. That he loved her, and she was his true wife. She always had been, and he wanted her always to be so....

Chapter Sixteen

'It is very kind of you to give me a ride into Buxton again, Lady Phaedra,' Catalina said as the carriage bounced down the road out of Castonbury. She had got up very early that morning, knowing that Phaedra was going on another horse-bound errand. She had to talk to Alicia again, alone this time.

'Not at all,' Phaedra answered. 'I am glad of the company, Mrs Moreno, especially since Lily is taking Miss Westman to visit her grandmother, Mrs Lovell, today. Though I am rather surprised you had an errand into town again so soon.'

'I have a friend there I must call on,' Catalina said.

'Indeed? A friend?' Phaedra arched her brow, and for an instant she looked so very much like

Jamie in his sceptical moments. 'You know, Mrs Moreno, you are most intriguing.'

Catalina laughed in surprise. 'Intriguing? Me? No, I assure you, I am very dull.'

'Just the chaperone who keeps to the background?' Phaedra shook her head. 'I don't think so. I think there is much more to you than that.'

'There is not,' Catalina said, wishing the Montagues were not so very observant. She *wanted* to be in the background. She wanted not to leave any mark on Castonbury.

'Everyone thinks I see only my horses, but that is not true,' Phaedra said. 'And I know my brother Jamie finds you intriguing as well.'

'Now that cannot be true,' Catalina protested.

'Why ever not? You are very pretty. Why should he not watch you?' Phaedra turned her head to stare silently out of the window for a moment. When she spoke again, it was almost wistful. 'I fear Jamie was a lonely man, even before he left for Spain. Being the heir, having so many expectations on one's shoulders, will do that, I suppose. But since he came home—I don't know. He seems in such pain. None of us can really reach him.'

She suddenly turned back to Catalina, her eyes solemn and direct. 'But when he looks at you, he smiles.'

Catalina closed her eyes against the pierce of hope and fear. She wanted so much to confess everything to Phaedra, but she knew she could not. 'He seems a very good man, Lady Phaedra. And—and he makes me smile as well. But I know he needs a different sort of wife than I could be. A proper English duchess.'

'Truly?' Phaedra cried. 'Oh, Mrs Moreno, you must know so little of our family. We never do anything in a "proper English" way. My sister Kate had a disastrous Season, and now she is married to a black man, a former American slave, and living in Boston. I had no Season at all, and you see how I live. Giles is marrying Lily, whose grandmother is a Gypsy and is welcome at our house. And Harry's Elena is Spanish, just as you are. Not to mention my father's illegitimate daughter.'

Catalina had to laugh at such a litany of scandal. It *did* make her fears sound small indeed. A product of growing up in a place where she never felt she really belonged. 'When you put it like that...'

Phaedra nodded. 'Jamie needs someone who can help him with the huge task of rebuilding and running Castonbury. Who can make him not brood so very much. Who can make him happy, as the rest of us are happy in our marriages. I don't know at all if that is you, but—well, if you like my brother, I hope you might give him a chance. He is a good man. That is all.'

Catalina nodded as she thought of what Phaedra had said, all the implications of those seemingly simple words that were not really so simple at all. 'You have given me so much to think about, Lady Phaedra.'

'Good. Then I can stop being interfering. It doesn't suit me so well, I fear.' The carriage slowed as it came into town and Phaedra glanced out of the window again. 'Shall I drop you outside the Assembly Rooms?'

'Yes, that would do well, thank you.' Once Catalina was alone on the walkway, watching the carriage roll away, she knew that what Phaedra had said was true. She had spent too long dwelling on reasons why she and Jamie should not be together. Yet what if there were reasons why they should be?

But first she had to be rid of the pernicious Webster. She looped her reticule closer about her wrist and turned towards Alicia's house. She glimpsed Alicia's pale face at one of the upstairs windows, but she quickly vanished when Catalina knocked at the door.

'Mrs Moreno,' she said, her voice full of surprise as she opened the door. 'How nice to see you again so soon.'

'I hope I am not calling at an inconvenient time,' Catalina said.

'Not at all. Please, do come in.' Alicia led her to the sitting room, where sewing things littered the table. She quickly swept them into their box. 'I'm afraid the maid is out, but I could probably make some tea.'

'No, please don't go to the trouble. I won't stay long,' Catalina said. 'Is your son here?'

'He is with my neighbour for the afternoon.'

'Has there been any trouble?'

Alicia shook her head. 'No, nothing at all. Crispin just likes to visit her, she is so kind to him. I begin to hope Webster has gone from here, after all.'

'That is not terribly likely, is it?' Catalina said. 'He has lost so much. If he is at all the same as he was in Spain, I doubt he would ever go so quietly.'

'I fear you are right,' Alicia said with a sigh. 'I was a fool for ever listening to him for a moment. But I was so desperate....'

'There was never a chance Jamie was your child's father, was there?' Catalina said quietly. She knew there was not, yet somehow she felt compelled to say it aloud. To have everything out in the open.

Alicia squeezed her eyes closed as her cheeks slowly turned red. 'No, of course not. He never looked at anyone but *you* in Spain, Mrs Moreno. I—well, I envied that way he would watch you whenever you were nearby. As if there was no one else in the world at all. But he was never anything but kind to me, as were you. You never deserved what we did, Webster and me. Not at all.'

She pushed herself to her feet and went to look out the window at the street below. 'Crispin's father was Colonel Chambers.'

'Chambers?' Catalina exclaimed. 'He was your lover?'

'Yes,' Alicia said miserably. 'He was kind to me as well. He liked to talk to me, as his wife had no time to listen to him at all. I was so very lonely, you see.'

Catalina nodded. She *did* see. She, too, had felt that terrible, cold sense of being alone in the world—when she had lost Jamie. When she thought he was gone for ever and there could never be understanding between them.

'I did not know I was pregnant until after he died,' Alicia went on. 'And of course Mrs Chambers dismissed me. I didn't know how to take care of myself and my child, or even how to get home.'

'And that's when Webster approached you,' Catalina said.

'Yes. I was sure I had no choice, I—all I can do now is say I am sorry. I can never make it up to Lord Hatherton and his family. I can only hope to…'

Suddenly there was the sound of glass shattering from somewhere in the house. Alicia's head whipped around, and Catalina jumped up from her chair.

'I thought you said your maid was gone?' she said.

'She is. Whatever could that be? This is such a quiet neighbourhood.' Alicia hurried to the door, and before Catalina could shout at her to stop, to lock it, she swung it open.

Everything happened in a swift, violent blur. Alicia had barely opened the door halfway when a large man shouldered it open hard, knocking her to the floor. He grabbed Catalina hard around the waist as she screamed. He clapped his gloved hand hard to her mouth, and she had a quick glimpse of blond hair and even features.

It was the footman from Castonbury, the one who had given her Jamie's note.

She heard someone else rush into the room, and the footman pressed his hand even harder to her mouth. She could hardly breathe, but the raw fear made her fight like a wild beast. She kicked at him through her skirts, ruing the fact that she wore delicate kid half-boots. She twisted her head to bite his hand.

'Crazy bitch,' the man shouted. He lifted her

up and forced her down onto the floor on her stomach.

'There was only supposed to be the one,' Catalina heard Webster say as she struggled to be free. There was a sickening crack when Webster slapped Alicia and she cried out. 'But this is even better. Hatherton is sure to come after the Spanish bitch. I knew something was up when I saw her at Castonbury.'

Catalina kicked back again, struggling to break the man's painful hold. The next thing she felt was a sharp, heavy pain quick against the back of her head. There was a shower of light behind her eyes, a strange stickiness on her skin. She thought she heard a scream coming from a long way away.

Then nothing.

Chapter Seventeen

'Catalina? Catalina, wake up. Please, please, wake up!'

The words seemed so blurry and faint. Catalina felt as if she was slowly crawling up through a dark, thick cloud. It pressed down on her head, as if to drag her back down into peaceful sleep, but somehow she knew she had to struggle against it. There seemed to be something she needed just beyond her weak grasp, and that voice pulled her up out of the beckoning darkness.

Painfully, she pried open her gritty eyes. Candlelight pierced her brain, so faint yet so very bright. Her head pounded as if a hundred drums beat inside of it.

'What is happening?' she said. Her throat felt so rough.

'Oh, thank goodness! You are alive.' Slowly a face swam into view above Catalina. Alicia's face. Her blonde hair straggled from its pins, and a bruise marred her cheek. 'I was so frightened. I couldn't bear for yet another person to be hurt because of me.'

Catalina winced, and found that she lay on a hard floor with her head resting on Alicia's knee. Wherever they were it felt cold and damp, and dark with just that one flickering candle.

Then it all came flooding back to her. The shattering glass at Alicia's house, Webster knocking her to the floor. They had been kidnapped by the very man they had been scheming to trap.

Catalina sat up too fast, wincing as pain rushed through her head. 'Are you hurt, Alicia? Did he...'

'Oh, no,' Alicia said quickly. 'He just knocked me out and somehow brought us here—wherever *here* is.'

Catalina pressed her fingertips to her temples and studied the dark room they were in. It was a place she knew—the sheepherder's cottage in the woods where Jamie had brought her the day they had both got caught in that terrible downpour. It was the cottage where they had made love in front of the fire. She slowly pushed herself to her feet and went to try the door. It was securely bolted from the outside.

'I am sure someone will find us very soon,' she said, trying to push down the fear rising inside of her. Panic did no good. She went to the shelves along the wall and pulled down some blankets. She handed one to Alicia and wrapped the other around herself. 'Surely two men can't take two unconscious women out of the house without someone seeing.'

Alicia nodded, but Catalina could see how pale and frightened she was. 'Thank heaven Crispin was with the neighbour today. My poor baby. If Webster had got him as well…' She broke off on a ragged sob.

Catalina sat back down next to her and put her arm around Alicia's trembling shoulders. 'All will be well, I am sure. Lady Phaedra knew I was coming to Buxton today, and when I do not make it back to Castonbury she will know something is amiss and will tell Jamie. He will make that *bastardo* Webster sorry he was ever born.'

Alicia nodded again. 'You—you do love him, don't you?'

'Yes,' Catalina whispered. 'I do love him.' And she realised those were the truest words she had ever spoken. She loved Jamie more than anything, and she always would. No matter what had happened in Spain, who he had worked for, how long they had been separated, he was her beautiful, kind, strong Jamie. She had been a fool to think she could ever go away from him again. The past was gone. They had both done what they had to do in times of desperation, but now they were through it.

Or so she had hoped.

'I am sure that is one reason Webster hates Lord Hatherton so much,' Alicia said.

'What do you mean?'

'Webster wanted you in Spain. Once, when they were foxed, he bragged to Colonel Chambers he would have you, and when the colonel laughed at him he was furious. But even Webster could see how you and Lord Hatherton looked at each other. It was just one more thing Hatherton had— family, money, position, women—that Webster could never hope for.'

'And he took his revenge once he thought Jamie was gone,' Catalina whispered.

'Yes. Once he was gone and could no longer fight—and beat—Webster. Webster is a coward. He would never confront someone he hated directly. But now—now Hatherton is back.'

'Webster is surely done for.'

'I only hope we get out of here to see it.' Alicia sat back against the wall and stared into the flickering flame of the candle. 'I loved Colonel Chambers too.'

'Did you?' Catalina said. She could see the truth of it in the sadness in Alicia's eyes, and she suddenly felt something she had never thought she would for the woman—sympathy.

'Yes. Not as you love Hatherton, perhaps, but in my own way. He was so kind to me, and for a while I wasn't lonely any longer.' Alicia hugged her knees closer. 'But I know he is truly gone for ever and I will never have another chance with him. Not as you have now with Hatherton.'

Catalina turned Alicia's words over in her mind. She and Jamie *did* have another chance, a miraculous chance to find each other again. She had been so foolish ever to push that away, even for good reasons. Love was a gift given to so few. She and Jamie had found it again, and she wouldn't let it go twice.

But before she could tell him that, before they could begin the rest of their lives afresh, she had to get out of this prison....

She studied their provisions. It wasn't much. A few charred sticks in the fireplace, the wooden shelves that appeared solidly bolted to the walls, the blankets. But there were also some pottery jugs lined up on the highest shelf. She turned to examine the bolted door.

'If Webster came back, he would have to come through that door, right?' Catalina said. 'There are no windows.'

'I suppose so,' Alicia said listlessly.

'Then maybe I have an idea.'

Alicia peered up at her warily. 'What sort of idea? I'm not so sure…'

'Oh, come, Alicia! Surely anything is better than just sitting here waiting,' Catalina exclaimed. 'Help me reach those jugs up there, and then we can bind one of the blankets over the doorway.'

'Oh!' A spark lit Alicia's eyes as she sat up and turned to the door. 'Yes, I see.'

'There are two of us, and hopefully when he

returns Webster will be alone, and leave that trai-
torous footman behind,' Catalina said as they attached the blanket on either side of the door in
a sort of rope. 'If we can trap him as he comes
in, we'll have a second to hit him over the head
with the jugs. Then we can lock him in and run
for help.'

And if it did not work—at least they had tried.
Catalina wasn't ever going to stop trying to get
back to Jamie. She had to tell him she was wrong,
that she loved him and that was all that mattered.
All that had ever mattered.

Once they were done with their task, they
crouched to either side of the door and waited.
It seemed like hours but was probably not very
long at all when Catalina heard the metallic grind
of a bar being lifted from outside the door. The
door swung back and a man in a rough grey coat
stalked into the room.

Catalina only had a glimpse of blond hair before she shouted, 'Now!'

Alicia brought her jug crashing down on his
head, and he collapsed to the floor, entangled
in the blanket. Catalina saw it was the footman
unconscious on the floor and not Webster, but

there was no time to think. She grabbed Alicia's hand and they ran out of the door. They were almost free of the clearing around the cottage, the sky growing dark around them, when Webster stepped out from behind a tree.

He caught Catalina around the waist and swung her off her feet. Her hand was torn from Alicia's.

'Run!' Catalina screamed, and Alicia took off as fast as she could. She quickly disappeared into the dusk, and Webster wrenched Catalina's arm hard behind her back until she gasped with the pain.

'You Spanish whore,' he said harshly, twisting even harder. 'You always have to be where you're not supposed to be. Just like in Spain. My quarrel was with Alicia, not you. But you'll do just as well to draw Hatherton out.'

Catalina remembered what Webster had tried to do in Spain, the horrible hot weight of his body on hers, and she kicked out at him as hard as she could. Through the cold haze of terror she hardly knew what she was doing, but she felt her teeth sink into his hand as he tried to silence her.

'Whore!' he shouted. He lifted her higher in his arms and carried her back into the cottage just as the footman staggered out. 'I'll deal with you later. I have to catch that bitch Alicia first.'

He shoved her into the room and slammed the door behind her. Before she could throw herself at it, she heard the bolt drop back heavily into place. As she sank to the floor, the stub of the candle flickered and threatened to go out, leaving her alone in the semi-darkness.

Alicia got away, she told herself. She would surely fetch help.

But in the meantime Catalina was by herself. She wrapped her arms around her waist and closed her eyes as she envisioned that day she had married Jamie in Spain. His hand in hers as he led her up the aisle, his smile as they promised themselves to each other. It had meant so much to her then; it had meant everything.

It still did. She only wanted the chance to tell him that.

She sank down onto the floor, her arms around her knees and began to sing in a shaky voice. *'Conde Niño, por amores es niño y pasó a la mar...'*

Chapter Eighteen

Jamie didn't like the feeling of disquiet that came over him as he looked up at Alicia's house. He wasn't sure what had urged him to come here, but when Lily told him that Catalina had gone into town again something had told him he had to follow her.

And now he was glad he had. The guard he had set on the house that day had vanished. Everything seemed just as quiet and peaceful as ever on the street, yet he knew so well how deceiving appearances could be.

On the way out of Castonbury he had seen William Everett and asked the man to meet him there at Alicia's house. He hadn't arrived yet, but Jamie took his pistol and dagger and climbed down from the curricle. He silently went up the front steps and found the door ajar.

Every muscle in his body tensed and went on alert. He nudged the door open with his boot and slipped inside.

He listened closely for any hint of noise, any slight rustle of movement, but there was nothing. The house was eerily silent.

'Catalina? Alicia?' he called. His voice echoed through the empty hall. He went through to the sitting room and heard the grind of broken glass under his boot.

In one frantic moment he saw the shattered window, the overturned furniture. Catalina's shawl on the floor. In the centre of the settee a dagger hilt was standing straight up. Jamie stumbled forward to find a note pinned under the blade.

If you want your whores back, Hatherton, go and get them at the old sheepherder's cottage in the woods. ...

'Lord Hatherton? Are you there? What has...' Everett appeared in the doorway, slightly out of breath as if he had run after Jamie. 'What has happened here?'

Jamie silently showed him the note, and Everett's sun-browned face turned pale. 'He has taken them, this man Webster?'

'To the hut at the edge of the woods,' Jamie said tightly. If that bastard Webster had been writing a melodramatic play he could not have chosen better than to take Catalina to the place where they had made love. Where they had finally found each other again. Now it was her prison.

But he would have her out of there soon enough. And then he would kill Webster.

He turned around silently and headed out of the shambles of the sitting room.

'I am coming with you, my lord,' Everett said, hurrying after him.

'It is me Webster is after,' Jamie said. 'I can't ask anyone else to go into danger.'

'You aren't asking me, my lord—I'm telling you,' Everett said stubbornly. 'I have to help her.'

Jamie turned to see the same burning fear and resolve he himself felt reflected in the estate manager's eyes. 'You care about Alicia.'

'I love her. And even if she won't have me, I have to help her now. To do anything I can for her.'

'So be it,' Jamie said with a nod. 'I am glad to have you with me, then. You are armed?'

Everett showed him the pistol he had tucked inside his coat. They hurried back to the carriage and Jamie urged the horse as fast as it could go back on the road out of town. They drove in grim silence, the evening gathering quickly in on them.

Until suddenly a pale figure darted out from the thick stand of trees by the side of the lane. It was a woman in a light blue dress, and she waved her arms frantically as she screamed his name.

'Lord Hatherton!' she cried. 'Oh, thank heaven you are here.'

'Alicia,' Everett shouted. He leapt down from the carriage even before Jamie could draw to a full stop and ran to catch her in his arms. She clung to his neck, sobbing. 'Are you hurt?'

'No, no, but—oh, Lord Hatherton, you must go after Catalina,' Alicia said. 'She distracted Webster so I could run away, but now she is trapped there.'

'In the cottage?' Jamie demanded.

'Yes,' Alicia choked out. 'I don't know if she is alone, or...'

Jamie didn't stop to hear any more. He knew he could move quicker now on foot than in the carriage, and he ran towards the pathway. He didn't even feel his injured leg any longer. He only knew he had to get to Catalina.

'Wait for me, my lord,' Everett called.

'No,' Jamie shouted back. 'You see to Alicia. Go to Castonbury for help.'

And he kept running until he glimpsed the cottage just ahead in the clearing. But he saw to his horror that it was in flames....

Catalina must have fallen asleep, she realised as she suddenly jerked awake. For an instant she felt dizzy and disoriented, as if caught in the sticky web of some dark nightmare. Her throat felt dry and raw, and something sharp and pungent was seeping into her nostrils.

Her eyes flew open, and she saw that the candle had toppled into a pile of blankets and flames were dancing up the wall. Smoke curled around her feet.

She leapt up and ran to the door, frantically trying to pull it open. It was still barred.

'Let me out!' she screamed, pounding on the door. She coughed on the smoke and pressed her arm over her face. *'Dejar yo fuera*, let me out!'

Was this the end, then? Had she survived everything in Spain only to die here? So many things flashed through her mind, Lydia and Mr Hale, Lily and Giles's wedding. The cool green fields and pale walls of Castonbury. Jamie and how very much she loved him. Were they all gone from her now?

'No,' she cried. No, she would not give up her life so easily. She had so much to live for. She had found Jamie again. She threw her whole body against the door. Pain shot down her side, but she ignored it and threw herself forward again and again until she sobbed in exhaustion.

Suddenly the door was flung open and she stumbled. She would have fallen if a pair of strong arms hadn't closed around her and lifted her up.

'Catalina!' Jamie shouted. 'My darling, are you hurt?'

She clung to him as she shook her head. 'I'm

not hurt,' she managed to choke out just as she heard timbers snapping in the roof.

Jamie spun around and ran with his love in his arms to the edge of the clearing. The night was terribly lit up with smoke and flames. He lowered her carefully to the grass and kissed her hard over and over. His gaze scanned over her as if to assure himself she was truly unhurt.

'Where is Alicia?' she asked.

'She is safe,' Jamie said. 'We found her running down the road. She and Everett have gone to fetch more help at Castonbury.'

'Oh, Jamie,' Catalina whispered, suddenly realising the enormity of what had almost happened. They had nearly been parted again, for ever this time. She couldn't quit shaking. 'I thought I might never see you again.'

Jamie held her close and kissed her forehead, her cheek, the corner of her mouth, over and over. 'I'll always come for you, my love. Always, no matter what. I promise you that.'

He kissed her once more and helped her to her feet. When her knees nearly buckled, he caught her around the waist and held her steady.

'Come,' he said. 'I should take you home now and send for the doctor.'

'No, I don't need a doctor,' Catalina protested, but she let him lead her into the stand of woods that led to the road.

But they did not get very far. A man suddenly stumbled out from behind a tree in the darkness. His coat was torn and his red hair tangled, yet Catalina could see the mad glitter of his eyes. It was Webster. And he held a pistol levelled on them.

Catalina's mouth went dry, and her heart pounded with a fresh rush of panic. She spun around hard, pulling Jamie with her, but the footman was behind them with another gun in his hand. His face was white and his breath was laboured as if his panic was even greater than hers. The gun wavered in his hand yet he held on to it.

'So you got my message, Hatherton,' Webster said with a terrible triumph in his voice. 'I knew if I just waited in the right place you would come to me. This is meant to be.'

Jamie's hand moved towards his coat, as if he hid weapons there.

'I wouldn't do that if I were you, Hatherton,'

Webster said. 'Not with my friend's gun aimed right at Mrs Moreno's pretty head. I'm sure you wouldn't want anything to happen to her, as it did in Spain.'

Jamie's arm tightened around Catalina. 'What is your game, Webster?' he said brusquely.

'I have no game here,' Webster said, his voice escalating. '*You* are the one who ruined my life by being alive, by exposing the plot I so carefully constructed around Miss Walters and her brat. You always did have a knack for using your un-earned privileges to ruin other people. But now it looks like I have the upper hand at last.'

Catalina glanced frantically between Webster and his footman accomplice. The man didn't seem to share Webster's wild confidence. The hand holding his gun trembled, which made the firearm wobble around in a terrifying way. What if it went off?

She was sure if she could catch him off guard she could knock him to the ground, leaving Jamie free to deal with Webster. But as she took a step towards him, the gun suddenly swung up and pointed at her face.

'Don't—don't come near me!' the footman screamed.

'Catalina,' she heard Jamie shout. He dragged her down just as a deafening explosion went off. The flames behind them crackled higher, and Jamie threw her to the ground, his own body over hers.

'Jamie! Are you shot?' She ran her hands desperately over his back and shoulders, searching for any wounds. She felt his breath on her skin, steady and warm.

'It's not me,' he said roughly as he pushed himself up over her. 'For God's sake, woman, what were you thinking, moving towards him like that? He could have killed you!'

'I thought I could distract him.' Catalina peered over Jamie's shoulder to see that it was the footman who had been shot. A pool of dark red blood spread over his chest as he toppled to the ground.

Webster still held the smoking pistol levelled in his hand. He shook his head with a horrible calm. 'That was regrettable, wasn't it? He was a useful ally for a time, but he was obviously losing his nerve.'

He tossed away the empty pistol and drew out

a dagger. As he took a step towards them, Jamie jumped to his feet and pulled Catalina up with him. He gave her a hard push and told her, 'Run, Catalina, now!'

She did as he told her—she ran. But she didn't go far. She could never leave Jamie. She snatched up the footman's gun from where it had fallen on the ground and dashed to the edge of the clearing, where she took what shelter she could behind a tree and tried to get a clear shot at Webster.

He and Jamie circled each other warily, their intent stares never wavering from each other. The glare from the fire glinted off the knives in their hands as Catalina's heart pounded with fear.

Suddenly, Webster lunged forward with his blade raised to strike. He let out a crazed, furious shout, but Jamie just slid agilely to the side. Jamie parried with his own dagger and drove Webster back.

And he kept driving him back, until he landed a strike on Webster's arm, raising a line of blood on his sleeve. With a cry, he lashed out hard with his foot to kick Jamie on his bad leg and sent him falling to the ground with a sickening thud.

Catalina cried out, but Jamie seized Webster's

wounded arm as he went down and dragged him along. They grappled heavily in the damp dirt, and Catalina couldn't see clearly what was happening. She heard grunts and dull thuds, barely audible over the crackle of the flames.

Webster's arm arced back to deliver a killing blow. Seeing the tip of the blade come to within an inch of Jamie's face, she screamed. But the sound strangled in her throat as Jamie twisted his assailant's arm sharply and pushed him off.

It was a horribly confusing scene in the firelight, a tangle of limbs and strikes and shouts. She couldn't see who was where, or get any kind of clear shot.

She fell to her knees with a frustrated sob just as Jamie's dagger thrust upwards and landed deep in Webster's chest. He fell face-first as Jamie rolled away, and then he was very still.

Jamie lurched to his feet to stare down at his fallen enemy, the man who had given them so much trouble. He carefully turned Webster over with his boot, and Catalina could see that he was truly dead. His eyes stared up at the night sky, glassy and sightless in the red light.

Jamie's face was completely blank, no triumph

or fear written there. Catalina dropped the heavy gun she held and ran to him, throwing her arms around his neck. She buried her face in his shoulder and held on to him as close as she could. He was alive! *They* were alive, and together at last. It hardly seemed possible after all that had happened.

But then she felt something warm and sticky on her skin, and swayed with a rush of dizziness. She suddenly remembered the blow to her head which she had forgot in the fight; it came back to her with a wave of cold nausea.

'Catalina!' she heard Jamie shout about the snap of the flames. Then she fell down into blackness.

Chapter Nineteen

'Conde Niño, por amores es niño y pasó a la mar...'

Catalina slowly opened her eyes and pulled herself up from the soft, dark cloud of sleep at the sound of a voice singing. It was not a sweet siren's song; the tone was cracked and dry, off-key. Yet she had never heard anything more beautiful. It made her want to struggle up out of the dreams that threatened to pull her back, even when pain pricked at the edges of her awareness.

But pain was as nothing compared to the hand that held on to hers. It made any torment of life worthwhile if she could just feel that touch for ever.

She opened her eyes to a piercing pale grey light. She was in her chamber at Castonbury, and rain pattered at the window. A tray sat on the bedside table, holding a pitcher of water, a bottle of some kind of medicine, a basin and a pile of cloths. The bedclothes were tucked around her, except for the hand that lay on the counterpane.

She slowly turned her head to find Jamie sitting by the bed. He slowly stroked her hand as he sang, his tousled head bent over her fingers. He looked rumpled and exhausted, his cravat loosened and his shirt wrinkled. He was the most beautiful sight she had ever seen.

'Jamie,' she whispered, and his head shot up.

'Catalina, you are awake,' he said. He raised her hand to his lips and kissed it. 'Are you in any pain at all?'

She tried to shake her head, but a jolt went up from the base of her neck to her eyes and she winced. 'A headache, that is all. But everything is a bit hazy to me. Is Webster…?'

'He is dead. He will not work his evil schemes on anyone else again.'

Catalina remembered it all then—Webster's body on the ground as the cottage burned down, his eyes staring sightlessly at the sky. She shivered, and Jamie's hand tightened on hers. 'No one else is hurt?'

'The footman is dead. Everett brought men from Castonbury, but by then it had begun to rain and the fire was going out. He helped me get you to the doctor.' Jamie's hand tightened on hers. 'Dear God, Catalina, but when you were so still and pale in my arms—I have never felt such fear. If I had lost you again…'

'But you did not!' Catalina covered his touch with her other hand and held on to him. 'I am here. We are *both* here. We have been given such a rare gift, and I—I was a fool to think I could ever turn away from it. I knew that when I was locked in the cottage. I love you, Jamie, *mi amor*. And I always will, even if you go away from me.'

'Go away from you?' Jamie said hoarsely. 'Never, Catalina. I love you too, more than my own life, more than anything. I felt dead inside when I lost you in Spain, and I never felt alive again until I saw you here at Castonbury.'

'You love me?' Catalina whispered, as a bright happiness like none she had ever known before bloomed in her heart.

'You are my true wife. Even if you left me and

I married someone else from duty, I would always long for *you*. For the other half of my heart. I thought having you as my wife would be the only practical solution—now I know it was only because I love you that I need you so much.' Jamie raised their linked hands, and Catalina saw that he had put her sapphire ring back on her finger. 'Will you marry me again, Catalina? Will you stay with me for ever, even as broken and scarred as I am?'

'Jamie, Jamie,' Catalina said. She was crying in earnest now. She couldn't stop the tears from falling as she threw her arms around his shoulders and held on as if she would never let him go. And she would not, never again. 'I would marry you a thousand times over. You are my miracle.'

'And you are mine.' Jamie held her against him, and to her shock she felt his own tears on her skin. 'We have been parted for much too long. I am never letting you out of my sight again. My wife, my love. My Catalina.'

'My Jamie. *Mi amor.*' And as they embraced each other, a ray of bright sunshine pierced the rain outside and the golden light shone down on Castonbury.

Epilogue

'Happy is the bride the sun shines on,' Catalina heard Lily's grandmother, Mrs Lovell, say as the doors of St Mary's church were thrown open and the bride appeared in a cloud of ivory satin and fine lace, pearls in her dark hair. The light that poured in after her could not rival the brilliance of her joyful smile as she looked down the aisle to her groom.

The church was filled with summer flowers gathered from the estate, brilliant bursts of white, yellow, pink and red that scented the air with the perfume of the Castonbury gardens. Every pew was filled, and there were even people standing in the side aisles, for no one wanted to miss the long-awaited marriage of Giles and Lily.

Catalina studied the congregation around her.

The duke and Mrs Landes-Fraser sat in the front pew with Lily's beloved grandmother, while Phaedra and Bram held hands beside them. Phaedra did not wear her riding habit, but a stylish gown and bonnet of pale blue and yellow. The duke's niece, Araminta, was there from her new home in Cambridgeshire with her handsome husband, Lord Antony. His sister, Claire, whose husband, the renowned chef and hotelier André du Valière, had come to make the grand wedding cake, sat behind them. Adam Stratton and his wife, Amber, a new-found Montague, sat with his mother Mrs Stratton, who also cried just a bit as she watched Giles marry at last.

All the Montague family was there to celebrate, except for Lady Kate, who had written her congratulations from Boston—along with the news that she was expecting her first child.

The vicar Reverend Seagrove, Lily's adoptive father, beamed from his place at the altar as Lily and Giles joined hands and stepped before him. The music from the organ swelled, but the bride and groom only had eyes for each other.

'Oh, Mrs Moreno, isn't it beautiful?' Lily whispered. Then she gasped. 'Oh, no! You are not Mrs Moreno now. You are Lady Hatherton.'

Catalina smiled as she felt Jamie, who stood on her other side, reach for her hand. Jamie—her husband, married twice now. They had said their vows by special licence last night in the drawing room at Castonbury, in a ceremony much quieter than this one. The duke, still in shock at the news of their 'betrothal,' had stayed in his chamber, but Lydia and Jamie's siblings had witnessed their vows.

Another marriage had also taken place, even quieter and more secret, in the vicarage. Mr Everett and Alicia had been wed, and were already gone to the far north of Scotland where Jamie had obtained a position for Everett at an estate. Alicia was forgiven by the Montagues in thanks for how she had helped Jamie catch Webster, but they did not want to see her ever again.

And after all the wedding festivities were concluded, Jamie was planning to travel to London to endorse Mr Hale's suit for Lydia's hand with her guardian. The young rector smiled at Lydia now from across the aisle, making her giggle and blush.

It was a lovely day indeed, Catalina thought as she watched the sun come through the windows. Mrs Lovell was right—happy was the bride the sun shone upon.

She smiled up at her husband, and he squeezed her hand as Lily said, 'I do.'

'I love you, Lady Hatherton,' he whispered.

'And I love you, Lord Hatherton,' she whispered back. 'Always and for ever.'

* * * * *

Read on to find out more about
Amanda McCabe
and the

CASTONBURY
PARK
A Regency Upstairs Downstairs

series…

Amanda McCabe wrote her first romance at the age of sixteen—a vast epic, starring all her friends as the characters, written secretly during algebra class. She's never since used algebra, but her books have been nominated for many awards, including the RITA®, *Romantic Times* Reviewers' Choice Award, the Booksellers Best, the National Readers' Choice Award and the Holt Medallion. She lives in Oklahoma, with a menagerie of two cats, a pug and a bossy miniature poodle, and loves dance classes, collecting cheesy travel souvenirs and watching the Food Network—even though she doesn't cook. Visit her at http://ammandamccabe.tripod.com and http://www.riskyregencies.blogspot.com

Previous novels by the same author:

TO CATCH A ROGUE*
TO DECEIVE A DUKE*
TO KISS A COUNT*
A NOTORIOUS WOMAN +
A SINFUL ALLIANCE +
HIGH SEAS STOWAWAY +
THE SHY DUCHESS
THE TAMING OF THE ROGUE

And in Mills & Boon® Historical *Undone!* eBooks:

SHIPWRECKED AND SEDUCED +
TO BED A LIBERTINE
THE MAID'S LOVER
TO COURT, CAPTURE AND CONQUER
GIRL IN THE BEADED MASK
UNLACING THE LADY IN WAITING
ONE WICKED CHRISTMAS

* *The Chase Muses* trilogy
+ linked by character

AUTHOR Q&A

Apart from your own, which other heroine did you empathise with the most?

That is such a hard question! I was really fascinated by everyone else's characters and the way they developed—both in their own stories and as characters in the series as a whole. I did really admire Phaedra in *Unbefitting a Lady*—she seemed like such a free spirit, determined to follow her own heart and passions wherever they would lead her. Plus, she was my hero's favourite baby sister!

Which Montague do you think Mrs Stratton the housekeeper let get away with the most?

I loved Mrs Stratton! She almost seemed like a second mother to the Montague children, watching them grow up and showing them affection when their own parents could not. I think maybe she had a soft spot for my hero, Jamie—he was the oldest and the most solemn (even when he was a child!), and she might have felt just a bit sorry for him...

Which stately home inspired Castonbury Park and why?

We decided to take Kedleston Hall as our model for Castonbury. It's a large, grand, built-to-impress house, unusual in many of its architectural features, and has extensive and beautiful grounds (with lots of places for secret romantic meetings!). There is a great deal of information and many images available and also several of the authors had visited, so it seemed like a good spot for our characters. (And in spirit it's a lot like Downton Abbey, a place that has its own character.)

Where did you get the inspiration for Jamie and Catalina?

I love the idea of wartime romance—a whirlwind, passionate affair surrounded by danger and uncertainty—and when Jamie first came into my mind I could see him as a man who would be surprised to find love at such a time and would be even more passionate for that. I also love the country of

Spain, its landscape and turbulent history, so I loved it when a Spanish heroine appeared who was perfect for him.

What are you researching for your forthcoming novel?

I am starting another Regency series, centred around a family at the centre of a small, almost *Cranford*-esque village! I can't give away too much about it yet, but I am loving the characters and the trouble they can get into in such an unexpected place...

What would you most like to have been doing in Regency times?

I think I would have loved to be doing just what I do now—writing stories! I have always loved the image of Jane Austen devising her stories in the midst of a busy Regency house, finding inspiration in the people and environment around her. But probably I would be scrubbing pots in the scullery...

AUTHOR NOTE

When I was first asked to take part in this project I was so excited! I loved the one collaborative project I'd done before (The Diamonds of Welbourne Manor with Diane Gaston and Deb Marlowe) and this one was even more extensive and involved. I would get to try a new writing method, as well as work with authors I've admired for a long time. Also, I am a huge *Downton Abbey* and *Upstairs, Downstairs* fan! The challenge and fun of creating a similar world in the Regency—a family and a house caught up in the tides of enormous change and scandal—was too much to resist. It was one of the most rewarding experiences I've found in writing to help build such a world.

I got the job of wrapping up the series with the last book: the tale of Jamie, Marquess of Hatherton, whose reappearance in his home after a mysterious absence of years throws Castonbury into chaos once again. I was worried about doing justice to the other characters, but I loved working with everyone else to bring their characters into my story and making them a part of Jamie's tale. And I have to admit I *adored* Jamie! I have always had a weakness for dark, tormented, complicated heroes who carry secrets in their hearts and when I found out that one of his secrets was a lost love —well, I just felt for him all the more. I loved seeing him find his way back to his family and his home and discovering how his experiences in wartime had changed him.

I was very inspired by diaries and letters from the time of the Peninsula campaign, where many British soldiers found romance with Spanish ladies. It was a turbulent, passionate time and Catalina was very much a part of all that. She was also more than a match for Jamie! It was the hardest thing I've ever written to tear them apart—but that just made it more fun to bring them back together again at Castonbury...

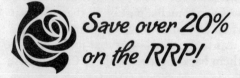